Restless
Dolly Maunder

OTHER BOOKS BY KATE GRENVILLE

Fiction
Bearded Ladies
Lilian's Story
Dreamhouse
Joan Makes History
Dark Places
The Idea of Perfection
The Secret River
The Lieutenant
Sarah Thornhill
A Room Made of Leaves

Non-fiction
The Writing Book
Making Stories (with Sue Woolfe)
Writing from Start to Finish
Searching for the Secret River
One Life: My Mother's Story
The Case Against Fragrance
Elizabeth Macarthur's Letters

Restless
Dolly Maunder

Kate
Grenville

CANONGATE

This paperback first published in Great Britain, the USA and Canada in
2024 by Canongate Books

First published in Great Britain, the USA and Canada in 2023
by Canongate Books Ltd, 14 High Street, Edinburgh EH1 1TE

Distributed in the USA by Publishers Group West
and in Canada by Publishers Group Canada

canongate.co.uk

2

First published in Australia by The Text Publishing Company,
Wurundjeri Country, Level 6, Royal Bank Chambers, 287 Collins Street,
Melbourne Victoria 3000 Australia

British Library Cataloguing-in-Publication Data
A catalogue record for this book is available on
request from the British Library

ISBN 978 1 80530 250 6

Book design Imogen Stubbs
Image of Dolly Maunder on p. 234 courtesy of Kate Grenville
Typeset by J&M Typesetting

Printed and bound in Great Britain by CPI Group (UK) Ltd,
Croydon CR0 4YY

Once more to Bruce
with love

1881

Currabubula, New South Wales

AS soon as she could walk, she knew she wanted to be outside, moving. The house was too dark, too small, smelling of stale woodsmoke and dogs. It was outside she wanted, the horizon shaped by the perfect cone of Duri Mountain on one side and the high ragged outcrop of Terrible Billy on the other. Outside, and moving around. The sky above you and the dirt under your feet, and always the shape of the land against the sky like a familiar face.

She was Sarah Catherine, but always called Dolly. She'd arrived into an already crowded family, five brothers and sisters before her and another brother coming along behind. Sophia was thirteen, her red curly hair like a shining river glinting with light when she undid it. Next down was Tom, his face made crooked by a bent eye. Their mother said it was because she'd been frightened by a bull when she was carrying him. Then Willie, everyone's favourite, always had time to give Dolly a ride on his shoulders. Rose was the kind sister, put Dolly's hair in papers, said she was the prettiest thing she'd ever seen. Eddie was close enough, only four years older, that sometimes he'd let Dolly tag along with him. Showed her how to catch a sheep, set a rabbit trap, milk a cow. Below her was the last child, Alfred, always known as Sonny.

They were six miles out of Currabubula, three dusty streets and a pub. She was five before she saw a town. Tamworth was twenty miles away and the Maunders didn't have much call to go there.

Dolly started life indulged and petted. The dolly. Her big sisters had to churn the butter, make the bread. She was always the little one, the one whose hands were too small to lift the milk pail or drive the churn through the cream. It was always easier for someone else to do it.

In Dolly's childhood there was Before Willie and After Willie. He was killed off a horse one morning, leaned down from the saddle to open the gate, the same way he'd done a hundred times, but the horse was fresh and bucked and threw him against the gatepost, and then trampled him, trampled his head with clumsy great iron hooves. The blood balled on the dust, glittering in the early sun, Dolly ran out with the rest and saw, and the flies coming to it as quickly as if they'd been waiting.

It shattered the world of the little house. After that everything was ugly and angry and sad. Dolly's mother went into a long silence, her face wooden, moving slowly like a person asleep, or wanting to be. In all the years After Willie, Dolly never saw her mother smile, only go about the endless tasks, banging open the stove door to throw in more wood and clanging it shut as if to punish it.

Dolly could see that her mother's life was just a lot of hard work. There wasn't often anything gentle in her voice, except when she went through the family story, telling over where she came from, where everyone fitted together, as if all the raggedness in her life could be knitted up into that laying-out of the generations.

Her mother's father had been John Martin Davis. Your Grandfather Davis, Dolly, she'd say, as though he might walk in the door, but he was long dead. He'd come from Ireland way back, a free settler, and set himself up beside the Currabubula creek. He'd married Sarah Wiseman, daughter of a thief-made-good who'd been *sent out*.

Everyone knew about old Granny Davis coming from *the taint*, but her children—*your Aunt Em, your Uncle Bob*—all married well. All except Dolly's mother. Each time she talked about her past she used the same words: *I married down*. That made no sense to Dolly, her father was a big man, taller than her mother, how could she have *married down*? But she didn't ask. There was something grim in her mother's voice when she said *I married down*, and as Dolly got older she could see what it must mean.

3

Thomas Maunder had been brought out from London as a poor Cockney boy to work on the huge sheep run near Curra called Goonoo Goonoo. It gave him a special bitter satisfaction to go over and over the stories of his humiliations there. How he'd been made to take three rams from Goonoo Goonoo over the open country to Quirindi—without a dog!—and him a boy fresh off the boat who'd never seen a sheep. Made to dig his own sister's grave when she died. Made to stand humbly with his hat in his hand while the boss Mr King called out, Stand back, my man! You harbour the flies so! Dolly's father told over the hurts like jewels, turning them in his memory so they flashed with his anger.

But he'd worked hard, boasted that in his younger days he'd held the shearing record in the area, 222 sheep in a single day with the blades, and finally got his own place, where they were now: Forest Farm.

Dolly never saw anything soft in her father. When he came in from the paddocks he filled the kitchen: massive, solid, a great rock. Sat at the head of the table, his big rough hands flat on the wood, waiting for his tea to be put down in front of him, and woe betide if it wasn't ready when he was.

Her father was a mystery to her, his rages and his strange jerky laugh, like a dog barking. Even when he'd had a few, he was always a hidden man. The only thing that softened him was telling over the streets and lanes of Home. The Old Country this, the Old Country that. Born within sound of Bow Bells, he'd boast. What he meant was, anyone born in Currabubula, New South Wales—which was everyone else around the table—wasn't worth a damn.

There'd been no schooling back in Shoreditch for Dolly's father. He could sign his name, that was about it. But Dolly's mother wrote a fair hand and could read most things, because Grandfather Davis had been an educated man and found a tutor, old Charles Job, to make sure his children had a bit of learning. So in the Maunder household it was Dolly's mother who did any reading or writing that had to be done, and it was her tricky task to save her husband's pride.

Her father sat at the table one night with some legal paper in front of him. Her mother was the one who could read, but her father was the man, so it was him had to sign it. She saw him take the pen in his unaccustomed hand and grind out his name onto the paper. He glanced up, saw her looking, and his face shifted under its wrinkles and whiskers in a way she'd never seen, some strong thing working away within him, knowing his little daughter was watching that labour with the pen.

They were all frightened of their father and his belt with the big brass buckle. The house was small, everyone around the table in the kitchen could hear it from the front room, that slap of leather on skin. The pressed-down feeling, no one looking at anyone else while they waited out the bad weather of their father's anger.

Now and again, though, at the end of a long day of shearing or getting the hay in, there'd be moments of rough warmth between the father and his sons. They'd all gone together at some mountain of work and beaten it, and one of them would say something over the stew that made the others laugh, something that had happened in the shearing shed or the paddock. But it was only for the pleasure of the men. They weren't going to explain the joke to the women.

Girls were of no account, you learned that early on. Good enough to make the bread and milk the cow, and later on you'd look after the children. But no woman was ever going to be part of the real business of the world.

◆

There'd never been a school in Curra, only old Mr Job who'd taught the Davis children. Once they grew up he'd made a few shillings every week teaching around the table in his room at the back of the pub, but he was too old now to manage a roomful of children. Then, the year before Dolly was born, a new law came in that said every child had to go to school till they were fourteen, and the government would pay for the school and the teacher. Dolly was a year old when Currabubula Public School opened.

Her older brothers and sisters went along till they turned fourteen. For Sophia and Tom that was just a couple of years, and even for Willie and Rose it wasn't for long. In any case, none of them went every day or even every week, only when their father could spare them. The farm ran on sheep, and in the days before fencing wire was cheap, if a man had sheep he had to have shepherds. *Children are cheaper than fences*. That was a joke their father liked. They were supposed to attend for the Required Number of Days, but easygoing Mr Goard at the school turned a blind eye, especially at shearing and harvest time.

By the time Dolly was school age, Mr Goard had been transferred down to Murrurundi. The new teacher, Mr Murray, was a different kind of man. One afternoon their neighbour Edwin Harper arrived at the kitchen door red in the face, sweating, swearing, shouting. Wouldn't sit, brushed away the cup of tea, paced up and down hitting the palm of his hand with his fist while he told the story. Pat Murray had dobbed him in! Got Constable Grant from Werris Creek to give him a bloody summons! He had to go before the judge in Tamworth next week for not sending the kids on the Required bloody Number of Days!

Her father poured Harper a whisky, agreeing yes, it was a shocking bloody thing. But with a thoughtful kind of look.

In the end Mr Harper had to go to court. Was found guilty, six children, a shilling fine for each one plus four and tenpence costs, and if the Harper children weren't ticked off on the school roll for the Required Number of Days in the future, next time it might be jail.

So from then on it wasn't a matter of going along to school when their father could spare them, it was every day up to the Required Number of Days. It was a fence run through the middle of the family: the older children who'd snatched what learning they could and now spent every day working, and the younger ones—Eddie and Dolly and Sonny—going off to school every day. One or other of the big brothers and sisters

7

opened the gate for them, lined up one behind the other on the pony. Watched them go, saying nothing.

◆

Currabubula Public School was a solid little square of brick with a house for the schoolmaster next to it. One room, fifty children aged from five to fourteen, long wooden benches. A smell of feet and the dripping on lunchtime bread, and the peppery smell of too many people in not enough air. Out the front, Mr Murray the teacher and Miss Thuell the pupil-teacher.

At school you could see exactly where everyone stood. At the top were Dolly's Davis cousins, whose parents hadn't *married down* the way her mother had. It was never spelled out, but known just the same, that no matter how many sheep Thomas Maunder could shear in a day, he'd never be as good as Mr Davis of the Davis Hotel. Yet those cousins and Dolly had the same grandfather, Grandfather Davis, and the same grandmother, Old Granny Davis, in her eighties now but still going strong, you couldn't kill her with a stick.

Dolly and her mother visited Granny Davis now and then, Dolly's face washed and the blue check pinny on. Old Granny Davis was blind, her eyes cloudy grey with red rims, but she wouldn't let anyone else pour the tea. Stuck a finger down the side of the cup so she'd know when to stop. Granny Davis's face was such a great age it seemed dark, all the wrinkles making a web of shadows. Blind or not, she always knew where the biscuits were, groped for Dolly's hand and pushed the biscuit into it.

Auntie Clara lived with Granny Davis and looked after her. Dolly would see them from the playground, Old Granny Davis sitting on the verandah with her knees apart under the black dress and Auntie Clara sitting beside her looking out at the dusty street. Auntie Clara was really a cousin, not an auntie, and she wasn't that much older than Dolly, but there she was, just sitting, hour after hour.

At school there were the Davis cousins, and the Dalys and the Murphys and the Howletts, and the ones who rode in from Piallaway, two or three together on a pony, their hair cut the same way by the same mother putting the same pudding-basin on each head in turn.

At the bottom of the pack were the children who came barefoot, their clothes patched till they couldn't be patched any more. Bert Russell was one of them. Only a piece of bread, no dripping, for his lunch, and his jacket cut down from a man's, all the buttons missing and a torn greasy rim around the collar.

Bert was nearly the same age as Dolly and got to wear Mr Murray's special star nearly as often as she did, so his place was next to hers on the long bench. She drew a careful chalk line on the desk so his elbow wouldn't jog hers as he wrote, and she agreed with her Davis cousins that he smelled.

The thing about Bert Russell and his brothers and sisters was that they didn't have a father. There was no man in the little house down by the creek. Mrs Russell was supposed to be a widow, but she was always big in front with another baby coming. Teddy Abbott's aunt was Mrs Clewes, who did the necessary when the women of Curra were brought to bed, so

Teddy knew the story, or thought he did.

Who's your dad, then, Bert? he taunted. Ain't got no father, have you, he taunted. Youse is all bastards.

Then one day, dancing around little Allan Russell, he shouted You're half a black, Allan Russell! Got a touch of the tarbrush!

And it was true that Allan Russell, a quiet boy, had dark hair and greeny eyes, and a bit of sun tanned him browner than tea. But Teddy never had a chance to say it again, because Bert was there in front of him. Quite calm, with no particular expression on his face, like a person patiently going at a cow to make it turn the right way. But merciless. At the end Teddy Abbott was sitting on the ground with a hand up to the side of his head, his mouth ajar and his eyes looking at nothing. But not a mark on him that he could go home and show anyone.

Jim Murphy was two years older than Dolly, so he sat on the bench behind her. A smiling sort of boy, didn't seem to mind that he hardly ever got the star. Every time she got it he'd lean down, his head next to hers, and draw a tiny star in the corner of her slate, and when she graduated to a workbook he drew a star in that too, even though you weren't supposed to write anything that wasn't work.

Dolly's best friend was Minnie Lewes whose father ran the general store. When your father ran the store, you got to know about people. Minnie always knew the back story, the secret. Who had to put everything on tick and then be chased for the money. Who were the charity cases, Mrs Lewes slipping a bag of broken biscuits across the counter to them, or the chips of bacon that no one was going to buy.

The charity cases were all women, women without a man. There was Bert's mother, worn-out-looking and gaunt in the face, and Mrs Tierney the widow, and poor Miss Trumper with her cats.

Mr Murray the teacher was a big man with a red beard and he spoke with such a strong Irish accent he was sometimes hard to follow. He didn't hold back on the punishments. They all watched when Mr Murray lost his temper with Abner Jones one hot afternoon and gave him a great backhand slap across the face, his whole man's weight behind it, and the silver ring he wore left a mark that you could see for a week.

Mr Murray's daughter Molly was one of the big girls when Dolly started at school. A couple of years later you had to call her *Miss Murray*, because now she was the pupil-teacher. She took the littlies, teaching them how to make their letters, and when they fell over she'd take them into the teacher's house to put a plaster on their knee.

She was a prim, thin, buttoned-up young woman, her clothes always smooth and tidy, her hair neat in its bun. When the inspector came she answered him clear and confident, Yes, Mr Parkinson sir. No, Mr Parkinson. When Dolly was ten, Miss Murray was put in charge of a small school down the road at Terrible Vale. She was just seventeen. Dolly would see her sometimes in the afternoon coming back on her pony, a serious young woman with round glasses from all that studying she'd had to do. By yourself, in charge of eighteen children, with the inspector coming to check on you twice a year: no wonder Miss Murray looked serious.

There was Miss Murray, running a school all on her own, managing all those children, with a salary and money in the bank. But she was the only woman Dolly knew who wasn't just at home all day, banging the stove door open and closed, heaving the wet sheets around on washday, milking the cow, and always a baby wailing from the crib in the corner. It was coming to Dolly slowly, like water seeping into sand: if you were born a girl that was the life you'd have to live. Unless you could find a way out.

✦

Dolly liked going to school. Was often the one picked out to parse the sentence on the board. *The sun and south wind had a dispute as to which was the stronger.* She drew an arrow to the word *sun* and wrote in small neat letters *sun, common noun third person number singular neuter nominative case.* Enjoyed the puzzle of long division, 39387463973045333 divided by 965, all the way down the page and the answer there at the bottom, and the way fractions could split and split again into their lowest common denominator and join up again. They started every day with Mental Arithmetic and then Dictation. Even the long words, and Mr Murray's Irish way of saying them, didn't puzzle her. *The disposition to avoid manual labour of any kind, the idea that it is degrading and the belief that greater respectability attaches to clerical employment, are the errors which too frequently mislead the young and mischievously influence their choice of occupation.*

Every week she got another verse of 'The Wreck of the Hesperus' off by heart. Loved having Mr Murray's little felt star pinned to her pinafore so often.

You're a quick study, Dolly Maunder, there's no doubt about it, Mr Murray told her one day, and she thought she'd burst with pride.

Mother could sometimes be soft, just for a moment, towards a daughter who wore the star so often. My clever little Dolly, she said. Oh my clever little Dolly. Smoothed her hair as she said it, but there was something in her voice, almost like regret, that made Dolly wonder, was there something wrong with being *clever little Dolly*?

Go on then Dolly, her father said out of nowhere one night, the dinner eaten, the lamp sputtering. Go on, show us what they're teaching you.

She never forgot it, everyone around the table watching her, Rose meeting her eyes in a funny way and shaking her head to say no, but Dolly was too little, too silly, too puffed up with pride in being a *quick study*, and somehow she thought her father really wanted to know.

It was the schooner Hesperus
That sailed the wintry sea;
And the skipper had taken his little daughter,
To bear him company.

She knew six verses by heart. She did the first verse, she did the second. What a pleasure, to have the words rolling out so obediently! How impressed everyone would be! She didn't look at her father but felt him watching as her voice rang out clearly into the silence. She was finishing the third verse when he leaned forward and slapped his hand hard on the table. The lamp jumped, salt flew out of its dish.

His voice was quiet, that dangerous quiet. So that's what you're learning, he said. What that fella Murray thinks is more important than you pulling your weight around the place. Leaving it all to your brothers and sisters.

She stared down at the table, at the grain of the wood, the dent where the big iron pot had fallen long ago and left the mark of its weight behind. She wished she was that wood, that grain. It seemed the silence would never end, everyone sitting as still in their chairs as if they were pictures of people.

It was her mother who rescued her.

Bed, Dolly, she said. Her voice had a rough edge as if her throat was being squeezed. Just go and get yourself to bed, quick now.

1896

A Dark Nothing

WHEN girls left school at fourteen they stayed at home helping their mothers until they got married. Dolly and Minnie agreed they'd had enough of kneading bread and washing sheets for a lifetime, but there weren't many other options. There was nursing or teaching, or if you were Catholic you could be a nun. That was it, pretty much, for girls from ordinary families in a little back-of-beyond place like Curra.

Minnie had a cousin who was a nurse. Dolly thought that might be all right. You'd wear the special uniform, people would call you Sister. But Minnie told her that her cousin was living in a dormitory, under Matron's thumb day and night. And the bedpans. Minnie had to tell Dolly what they were. Oh, no thank you!

By the time Dolly and Minnie were twelve, they'd made up their minds that they'd be teachers like Miss Murray. You applied to be a pupil-teacher and sat for an exam. You'd have to get the train to Tamworth for that, it would be all afternoon, she'd have to stay the night at Uncle George Maunder's. She'd pass, of course she would. Then she'd do another year, and do the next exam, and the next. They got harder, she knew. Not just any old person could be a teacher! Then you applied for a job as junior teacher at a big school, or a small school of your own, the way Molly Murray was at Terrible Vale.

Dolly and Minnie had it all planned out. They'd have a neat black skirt like Miss Murray's, and a watch like hers pinned to their blouse. They'd learn how to write on the blackboard so the chalk didn't squeak and how to look at a child so they did what they were told.

After that the picture was a bit vague. Dolly and Minnie knew they'd end up getting married, because you wouldn't want to spend your life as a spinster like Miss Trumper. And you couldn't go on teaching forever, because the law said that a married woman wasn't allowed to have a government job. But until you had to give it up you could have some fun. You'd get away from home and you could look around a bit. You might meet young men of a different kind from the boys around Curra. And you'd have money of your own and a place in the world.

✦

No one stayed at school a day after they turned fourteen. That final year, you just sat at the back of the room doing work you'd done before, marking time till your birthday. No one Dolly knew had gone to high school. You had to pass a hard exam, and even if you did, the nearest high school was two hundred miles away.

Minnie turned fourteen and left school that afternoon. She had an uncle over the mountains in Dorrigo and his wife was poorly. It had been arranged that Minnie was to go and live with them and help out. Dorrigo was a long way, and an awkward place to get to from Curra. Saying goodbye, Dolly knew she wouldn't see much more of her friend. In any case, Minnie had changed. She'd once been so bold and sure about the pupil-teacher thing, but in the last few months she'd gone quiet about it. She hugged Dolly on the station platform and said how much she'd miss her, but she got on the train eagerly enough, leaned out the window and waved her hanky as if it was a great adventure. It seemed that she'd forgotten all her brave talk.

Then Dolly was coming up to her fourteenth birthday. The week before, she plucked up courage to ask Mr Murray how you went about applying to be a pupil-teacher. Waited back after the other children left. Mr Murray was in a hurry, he needed to get his cows in to be milked, she could hear them bellowing outside. Ah, well now Dolly, he said, the first thing would be to ask your father, he'd have to give his permission. Then I'd have a word with Inspector Parkinson. Get your father to come and see me, Dolly.

Dolly wanted to say, Wait, no, but Mr Murray had his hand on the latch holding the door open for her to go out before him, and he was already calling to his son, Get that cow into the bail for me, Sydney, look sharp now lad!

All the way home she told herself, bide your time, Dolly, bide your time. She'd have to come at her father the right way, at the right moment. But what would be the right way, when would be the right moment?

There was no biding her time, in any case. That night at tea she watched her father take up his knife and fork like weapons, the way he did, holding them upright on either side of his plate, telling Rose she'd burned the onions, and couldn't she even give a man a decent dinner? Then he turned to Dolly. You'll be in the kitchen with your mother now, he said. I'll be needing Rose and Sophia with the sheep.

He put the knife down, smoothed the blade with a finger, and they all knew a joke was coming. Two girls, he said. Nearly as good as one man.

There'd be no other time, no way to find the right words.

I talked to Mr Murray, she said.

The kitchen had suddenly gone very quiet, even the fire in the stove listening.

About pupil-teaching. Her voice had gone wispy and strange. He said he'd have a word with the inspector.

Her father didn't have to be angry, didn't have to shout. When you were king you could keep your voice very steady, very quiet. Over my dead body, he said, as calmly as if he was asking for a slice of bread.

It was worse than if he'd shouted.

Over my dead body any daughter of mine goes out to work.

Goes out to work. In her father's mouth the phrase sounded outlandish, something a Hottentot heathen in Africa might do but not someone in Currabubula, New South Wales.

Who was there to stand beside her? Not her mother, not those brothers and sisters who were nearly strangers. No one at that table would go against Father.

The silence was defeating her, she wanted to throw words at it to make it go away. Took a breath, but watching her father, now forking up a great lump of mutton, she had no words. He looked around at each face one by one, his mouth turned down in contempt. Out to work! he said. And have every man point the finger and say I can't support my family!

Everyone was looking down, waiting for it to be over. His voice filled the room, there was no space for any other.

No more of this, girl, he said, pointing his knife at Dolly. Not another word.

Put the huge forkful of meat in his mouth, chewed away as if it was a hard duty put before him that he would grind his way through, like every other hard thing that had ever been put before him.

✦

At dry old Forest Farm the Maunders never stopped. Sunrise to sunset, seven days a week, the men out all day with the sheep or the crops, and the women—Dolly one of them now—in the kitchen and the washhouse.

In summer the day revolved around the heat. You got up early and opened the shutters to let in air that was cool from the night. Later you closed everything up, retreated to some dim place inside the house if you could, and hunkered down through the hours of heat. Outside beyond the dimness were the paddocks, the grass dry as straw, the sheep lying under the trees, shifting to follow the small patch of shade. During endless afternoons the great unfriendly eye of the sun seemed stuck in the same quadrant of the sky, as if it had no intention of ever sliding down towards the horizon.

Then suddenly it would be low, the shadows long, the light like honey, thick and sideways. Men and sheep would move again, birds making noises, dogs stirring themselves and scratching their ears, looking out with bright eyes at where they could smell the kangaroos. But such a short time! Between the hammer blows of the afternoon and the sudden darkness of night, there was no more than an hour or two when life was pleasant.

In winter it was dark when you got up and riddled out the stove, dark again by the time you dished up the tea. The mud out in the yard oozed up cold through the split wooden pattens.

It was Dolly's job now to set the bread every night and get the yeast bottle ready for the next day. Mix and knead till her wrists ached, three or four loaves, twice as many at harvest and shearing with all the hired men out on the paddocks. Rose had never had any trouble with the yeast but the damn stuff sometimes up and died on Dolly, too hot by the fire overnight or too cold if it was too far away from it, she supposed. When the bread didn't rise her father took the strap to her. There was something very shameful about being whipped, the way he'd whip a dog that was doing the wrong thing. Not much I ask you to do, missy, he'd say in that bitten-off way, the London vowels a threat in themselves. Just make us the bread, and you can't even do that.

There were often men working on the farm for Dolly's father and they all had to have plenty to eat. That meant three cooked meals every day for eight or ten men. They were working hard, needed a good feed, chops and eggs and great mountains of bread and butter. And twice a day, morning and afternoon, the scones and fruitcakes and billies of tea had to be taken out to where the men were working in the sheds or the paddocks, and if you forgot the sugar it was all the way back to the house, because the men wouldn't drink their tea without sugar. Then you'd see all your work gone in a few minutes of those big hungry men grabbing for the scones and slurping down their tea.

But before you could put the butter on the bread you had to churn the cream, and before you could churn the cream the milk had to be set out in the pans to separate, and before that the cow had to be milked, and before you could milk the cow you had to catch her and fetch her in, and fill up the food trough to keep her quiet while you milked her, and the bucket had to be scoured, and that meant getting the water hot on the back of the stove, and that meant lugging the water in. Then, in the evening, the whole thing all over again, and if you were late the cows let you know about it, and if the milk was off or the butter didn't churn properly everyone around the table would let you know about it too.

And before you could do any of that, the scones or the meat or the hot water, you had to get the fire going, and before you could do that you had to riddle out yesterday's ashes, a filthy job. No matter how much care you took, you'd end up with soot all over yourself. Fill up the wood basket and go out to the chopping block for the little pieces to get it going, and before there were any little chips to find you had to chivvy some man to split the wood, or do it yourself with your long skirt getting in the way, because if the stove went cold and there was no fruitcake and no tea, there'd be everyone around the table grizzling at you. No one was going to blame the man who'd forgotten to cut the wood and bring it in.

Washday was the worst, two big tubs outside. First you had to pump the water up from the underground tank into the buckets, pushing and pulling on the worn iron handle, then lugging each bucketful over to the tubs and setting the whole business up, the washing board, the wringer, the coarse yellow soap. But before that you had to have made the soap, that was a dreadful smelly job with the tallow and the lye bubbling away for hours, and then you had to stack the big cubes of it in the laundry, but the rats got to it no matter how carefully you wrapped it in canvas and put it up on a high shelf. Those damned rats ate right through the wall from the outside and got to it. You went to get another cake of soap to grate up on washday and it would be eaten away from behind and rat dirt everywhere.

The washing was a backbreaking job, the sheets and towels

full of water nearly too heavy to lift up to the wringer. It took two of you to manage the big things, and if a corner dropped on the dirt it had to go back in the water. Even when the things had gone through the wringer, the weight of them was still enough to pull your arms out of their sockets. Getting them up on the line, and pushing the clothes-prop under the line to lift everything up off the dirt, that took two of you, or Sophia, near as strong as a man. She was the only one could do the clothes-prop with a full load on her own.

Never enough water, the tank not big enough and the creek just puddles a lot of the year, so every drop of water had to be saved. If it was too dirty it went on the vegetable garden, and if it was cleaner it would do for someone to wash in. Washing day and ironing day, there was no time to cook food, the men had to make do with cold meat and a few potatoes, bread and jam, something like that, so you'd have to make sure there was enough left over from the Sunday.

Everything had to be done at once. You'd be getting the scones and the biscuits on while you were clearing away from breakfast, and the new jam boiling on the back of the stove and the potatoes for dinner waiting to be peeled. Always Father with never a word for when you did things right but a slap around the head when you didn't. Everywhere there was the cow shit, the sheep shit, and the smell of their own shit too, from the long-drop privy not far enough away.

It was a matter of trudging through the days, one coarse dirty job after another. The worst of it was the sameness. The same stove to be riddled out and get full of ash again, the same table to be cleaned down and get dirty again, the same pots to be scrubbed, and dirtied again, and scrubbed again. Every day that old basin with the mottled glaze and the big lip where you poured out the cake batter, every day another great thick fruitcake to take out to the paddocks. There were mornings when Dolly woke up and thought that if she had to look at it all again she'd rather die.

But there was no choice about that or anything else. By dawn Rose and Sophia would already be stirring in the little room they shared. Rose would shake her by the shoulder. Come along pet, she'd say, time to get up, dear, and then it would be Sophia, whipping back the bedclothes and telling her she was a lazy so-and-so.

The sisters whispered together at night in the room they all shared, Rose and Sophia together in one bed and Dolly in the little stretcher under the window. Complaining about Father, how hard he worked them, that was normal for all the girls they knew, but not every father was as mean as theirs was, two years since they'd had a new dress or a new pair of shoes, and even when he gave them a bit of pocket money he doled it out with bad grace.

Sophia and Rose would rouse on her for being lazy and spoiled and sneaking out of doing her fair share. Don't think we don't notice, Dolly Maunder! It was true, she sneaked out of work when she could. She felt sick, she had a headache. She had her time of the month, she had a sore foot. She hated her sisters for putting up with it. They complained, but it was the way you might complain about the rain or the cold. Sometimes she thought they were no better than the cows in the paddock, heads down, trudging through their days, their hands big and red and rough, their cheeks coarsened from the frosty mornings milking. She hated her sisters then, as you hate the thing you can see you're going to become.

There was a dark nothing where pupil-teaching had been. She didn't want to look at it. Lived night and day with the great lump of sorrow in her chest for the thing she wanted, the thing she ought to have, the thing she was made for: being in a schoolroom, the faces of the children turned towards her, explaining something so they understood it. On those dawn mornings she wanted to stay under the blanket, turn her face to the wall, watch the splinters do nothing, the way she was doing nothing, her self shrunk down to something lifeless.

Mr Murray had given her a book on her last day, *A Child's Garden of Verses*. It was the only book in the house, and for a while she hid herself away in the back of the cowshed and warmed herself at it, afraid she might forget how to read. But after a while she knew the words too well, and what was the point of keeping in practice? She'd never have to know how to read. There was nothing ahead of her except getting married, housekeeping for some man, and having children one after the other.

She slipped the book away behind a beam in the cowshed. That dream of schoolteachering was over. No point torturing herself thinking about it.

✦

Dolly's father had said he was going to take on another hand, and Bert Russell turned up one afternoon at the back door. He was seventeen, the same as Dolly. That shabby barefoot boy had grown into a tall man, all muscle, big around the shoulders from hiring himself out on farms since he'd left school. He had a smart well-trimmed moustache, a new white shirt, a fancy waistcoat. Looked at Dolly across the table, a bit shamefaced she thought, because she'd known him as that smelly hungry boy and now here he was sitting among her family, with her mother welcoming him. Come on, Bert dear, another scone, look, here's one with your name on it.

Bert filled the place where there was always the sad ghost of her mother's darling Willie, killed that stark dreadful day. No one can cure and slice the bacon the way I like it, only Bert, she'd say, and ruffle his hair as she passed behind his chair. He'd turn and give her that nice smile he had, and he was good to her in a thousand little ways. Quietly bringing in another load of wood for the kitchen stove, just the right size, not too big, not too small. Come washday, Dolly's mother would find the copper already filled, the firewood laid under it. And of course there was always the bacon, cured and sliced the way she liked it.

Dolly had a pretty fair idea now about what must have happened to Bert's mother. There might have been a Mr Russell once, but if so he'd died. Or maybe just taken off. Men did that. Then the only way Mrs Russell could feed herself and her children was to join up with some other man. But after a while there'd be another child on the way, and the fellow would take fright and make himself scarce. Then there'd have to be another man, and another baby coming.

Mrs Russell had been lucky in the end. A fellow called Henry Newitt had come along and he was sticking by her. He'd taken on all Mary Russell's children as well as having another brood of his own with her. Bert was ten when Henry Newitt came to live with them and became his stepfather.

Not that Henry Newitt brought wealth to that little house by the creek. He was a labourer, turned his hand to any kind of job, was even prepared to do the work no one else wanted. They all watched from the road one day as Henry Newitt cleaned out the long-drops at the school, first the boys', then the girls', then the one for the Murrays. The smell came to them on the breeze. Mr Newitt knew they were watching, never glanced around at them. Bert and his brothers were nowhere to be seen.

That was what Bert came from, and Dolly could see he wasn't going to let an opportunity slip by. Didn't mind buttering up Mr and Mrs Maunder. Sucked up to Dolly too, telling her how her scones were the lightest he'd ever eaten, and how she had a way with a spud like he'd never tasted.

Dolly wasn't fooled. She'd never liked Bert Russell and now he was too flash by half. She didn't draw a chalk line on the table between them, but there was one just the same. She'd won the star, week after week. But what good did that do her, when she was stuck here with these people, Dolly Maunder who could have gone schoolteachering?

Her father was as pleased as her mother to have Bert there. He could shear as well as her father could. In fact Dolly watched them up in the shed one day and wondered if Bert might have been holding back, not to put the older man to shame. Could lay a line of fence quicker than you'd credit, her father said, and had a way with the Clydesdales so they pulled a nice straight furrow behind the plough.

As well as owning Forest Farm, over the years Dolly's father had bought other properties, all within fifty miles of Curra: at Bellatta, at Attunga, at Gunnedah. When he needed a reliable man to supervise shearing or harvesting on those other places, he'd send Bert off. He came to depend on the younger man. They'd chew away at their mutton at the table, working out the best way to do things, Bert calling him Mr Maunder and letting him think it was his idea to try oats in that bottom paddock.

Bert caught her looking at him, saw the curl of her lip.

Ah Dolly, you were always the clever one, he said. Got the star that many times, old Murray had to give someone else a go.

He knew she didn't want him there, having her mother smile at him and her father listen to him the way he'd never in his life listen to Dolly. He was trying to make things right with her, but he'd picked a bad way to do it. He wasn't to know, but he'd put his finger on the place that hurt, and made it hurt all over again.

Oh, that old star thing, she said, casually, as if she couldn't have cared less. Well, you got it once or twice yourself if I remember. Not that big a thing to get the star.

She smiled because everyone was looking, but she wanted him to know she could see through him. Don't come flattering me, Bert Russell, she thought.

She put a hard look on her face, because inside she was sorry she'd said it. She'd thrown something away, something private and precious. Mr Murray's star *had* been a big thing. She'd cheapened the memory of the star, and what it had meant to her.

◆

Aunt Emma, one of her mother's sisters, had married well and lived on a property called Glendon near Bendemeer, in the high country fifty miles to the north. Now and then Dolly and her sisters were invited up there.

Glendon was a sprawling house with a curving driveway and a wide verandah all round. Little triangular gables in the roof, the rooms filled with light and space. Everything in the house was done nicely. There was no crowding round the kitchen table for their meals. At Glendon there was a big dining room, a great gleaming spread of dark mahogany, the white tablecloth changed every other day, knives and forks not solid silver of course, but good plate, and kept polished. No business about the pot of stew being put on the table. Everything was served nicely, in proper dishes, with big silver spoons to help yourself, and a starched linen napkin in a silver napkin ring beside your plate.

It wasn't Aunt Emma's daughters washing those napkins and starching them. Dolly never got the hang of how many people were working out the back of the house, but there was a cook and a kitchen maid, there might have been a couple of kitchen maids, and there was a parlourmaid and a woman who did the rough, and a silent dark man who split the wood and stacked it beside the fireplaces.

Dolly knew her father didn't like them visiting Aunt Emma. There was a deep wordless rage in him that the Davis family thought he was of no account, even though not a one of them could shear a sheep or split a fencepost.

He didn't let all the girls go at once, so it was two by two, and that meant Dolly had a room of her own, one of those little attic rooms, a neat bed with a lovely pink eiderdown on it, and the floor gleaming with beeswax polish between the clean rugs.

At Glendon there was plenty of water and they had a beautiful orchard and vegetable garden and the grapes were magnificent. The first time she went there to stay, she saw a dish of grapes on the table and reached out and picked a few off. Aunt Emma was kind enough, but made it clear that wouldn't do. 'Eat what you want, child, but cut a sprig, don't pick one or two off and spoil the bunch.' *Spoil the bunch!* That was a new idea, and there was even a dainty pair of scissors, grape scissors, made just for cutting off a bunch that you put on your side-plate. Then you put the scissors back in their special place under the fruit bowl.

Now you know the right way to do it, Dolly dear, Aunt Emma said. Which was a criticism, of course, of how things were done at the Maunders'.

Rose and Sophia grizzled about Aunt Emma behind her back, thought she was stuck up, sniggered about the grape scissors. They felt belittled by the place. Didn't want to learn about snipping a sprig off and not *spoiling the bunch*. Oh, that's just silly stuck-up nonsense, they said, and Dolly knew that they were jealous, only pretending not to be.

Dolly loved knowing about the grape scissors. It wasn't that she hankered after *nice things* to impress people. It was a bit ridiculous, when you thought about it, a special pair of scissors just for cutting grapes. It was that the scissors and the grapes and the napkins and everything else told her something important: there was a world beyond the one she knew. Something beyond the Maunders sitting glum around their old table, beyond dusty little Curra where everything was rough, coarse, dirty, half-broken, a life of hard work and nothing to show for it. It was a kind of hope. Even a kind of promise.

1900

Trying on Names

THE year the century turned, Dolly was nineteen. She'd never be exactly beautiful, she knew, but she was pretty enough. There was a dance at Howlett's Hall. And, fancy, it was written up in the *Freeman*. It wasn't often that Curra got a mention in one of the Sydney papers.

Currabubula: On the evening of Wednesday, July 24, a grand concert and ball was held in Howlett's Hall.

I have not time now, nor has the 'Freeman' space to particularize all the ladies' dresses, but as an unprotected male, living in a remote and lawless district, I must, from motives of personal safety, describe a few, and start with

Miss Dolly Maunder, who was attired in a white flow-ered silk, trimmed with white silk lace and blush roses; Miss Mary B. Daly, white nun's veiling, trimmed with turquoise blue and pink roses; Miss Digman, pale green nun's veiling, cream trimming, pink roses; Miss Minnie Lewes, pale blue satin, trimmed with pearl passementerie and pink roses: in fact all the dresses in the room were pretty and becoming, but my time forbids more than passing notice.

The fellow from the *Freeman* had given her the eye right from the start, an ugly sort of reddish older fellow but with an amusing satirical way about him. He'd come over to where the girls were standing, asked her for a dance, and she was pleased to have been singled out by a clever city fellow. He was a good dancer, pressing his hand into her back hard and authoritative. She'd never danced with anyone like that, so different from the timid local boys who seemed to think you might break.

Speaking close into her ear, he told her was going to write about the dance for the paper, and would she be kind enough to tell him how to describe the various lovely dresses of the various lovely young women?

Otherwise, he said, as an unprotected male in a remote and lawless district, I could not be sure of my personal safety!

She laughed and did her best to come back at him with something a bit lively.

All right, she said, but mind you mention mine first. And best!

It wasn't much, but he laughed, and Dolly felt herself expand into the words she'd surprised herself by coming out with. It was as if there was another person inside the Dolly Maunder she'd always known, someone pert and knowing, who had been sprung out of her hiding place by this ugly interesting man.

And now there she was, first on his list, and there was the little quip about being an unprotected male. He'd tried it out on her and she'd laughed, and now he'd used it in the piece.

Having her name in the paper, making a man like that laugh and look at her admiringly, made her feel—what?— interesting, admirable, desirable. So when she met Tom Connolly at the tennis party out at the Dalys', it gave her a sparkle. Tom Connolly was visiting from forty miles down the way at Murrurundi. His father was the big man down there, the way her uncle Bob Davis was the big man in Currabubula. Tom had a thick curve of hair that came down over his forehead and all afternoon, talking and joshing with him, pairing up for doubles, watching him over the rim of her glass of lemonade, she wanted to touch that hair, see if it was as soft under the hand as it looked.

And, oh yes, he was watching her too. She'd catch his eye and he'd smile his slow nice smile.

He was staying out of town on the Dalys' place, Patrick Daly was some family connection. Helping with the sheep, he said. Dad's of the view every man comes at his sheep in a bit of a different way, and Uncle Pat might have a trick or two he can let me in on.

Tom Connolly would get a good spread from his father, there was a place at Willow Tree, apparently, that would be his in due course.

There wasn't much in Curra to show a visitor, but there was cray-bobbing in the creek, and that made enough of a story for them to go down there the next day, a whole group at the start with Sonny and Teddy Abbott and Gert Daly. One way and another Tom and Dolly let the others wander further down the creek until it was just the two of them at the big rock beside the waterhole. They kept on pretending to be interested in the cray-bobbing, but as the shadows grew long and sloped away down the rock, and she knew the slanting sun was lighting up her hair, she could tell from the way Tom was looking at her that he wasn't thinking about yabbies, and neither was she.

He was only twenty, her own age. They were born exactly a week apart, they'd discovered, and that had some kind of importance to it. She tried it out to herself: *Dolly Connolly*. It had a bit of a strange ring, and for the first time she tried on her other names. *Sarah Catherine Connolly*. Ah, now that had heft. When the others came looking for them it was like the breaking of a dream.

There was the cray-bobbing, and there was the tennis, and there was a big picnic for everyone out at the Scotts'. Then all at once it was over. Tom went back to Murrurundi. He wrote a stiff little note, he'd been glad to make her acquaintance, and if ever she was passing through Murrurundi he and his family would always be pleased to see her.

It was the brush-off. Like a bit of fluff off your shoulder, she'd just been brushed out of Tom Connolly's life.

Gert Daly would have known the story, but Dolly was too proud to ask. She worked it out for herself. Turned out that Tom Connolly's uncle was a member of parliament, and he had a cousin married to a judge. That was what you called *well bred*, as if a person was a prize ram. And there she was, little Dolly Maunder, her father a shearer made good. Tom Connolly had liked her right enough. But Dolly was the wrong sort of family, and Tom's Uncle Patrick must have heard about the cray-bobbing and sent him back to Murrurundi quick smart.

Tom had kissed her that day with the sun tangling in her hair and they'd sat there watching the water with their hands together. He might not have wanted to go back to Murrurundi, but the stiff little note had said it all: the world I'm part of has no place for you, Dolly Maunder. His life had curved in towards hers, just for that moment, but curved away again like railway tracks, two sets of rails travelling towards different places.

She was hurt, it was a pain in the chest, an ache in the heart, but pretty soon where the hurt had been there grew a kind of rage. How dare you, Tom Connolly, how dare you.

For the first time in her life she thought about her father in a different way. *You harbour the flies so.* He'd been younger than she was now, only seventeen, when he'd been sent out from London, and look at him, by nothing but his own hard work he'd got Forest Farm and the other properties. His children would never go without.

It's made you a cranky old bugger, she thought. But you did it with no help from anyone. That's the stock I come from.

That's the *breeding* I've got. I'm not going to be ashamed of that.

She never tried on her other names again. *Sarah Catherine.* No, she was who she was, plain old Dolly Maunder.

✦

She'd always liked Jim Murphy at school, his slow smile and the little stars he'd done on her slate. When he turned fourteen he'd gone somewhere out Breeza way to work for his uncle and she hadn't seen him. But then one day she was in Curra at Lewes' store and there he was, looping the reins of his horse over the post.

He was a man now, tall in his riding boots and strong under his shirt, but when he saw her he gave her the same warm private smile he'd always given her when they were children together. Looked at her face, each bit separately, as if to remember the girl she'd been and compare it to the woman she was now.

He was at Lewes' most weeks after that, went with her part of the way home. They'd stop by the creek. There was a thicket of trees that was a sweet spot to sit with a smiling man holding her hand. One day, out of a long silence, he said, You're glorious, Dolly!

In that quiet glade, the horses nearby, their harnesses jingling when they shifted, they lay on the grass with the small secretive rustling of leaves all around. They came as close as they dared. Just a layer or two of cloth between them. She might have taken the risk, but he wouldn't.

What's the harm, Jim, she said, just doing the natural?

But he said, Dolly, oh Dolly, it's my eternal soul.

What soul, she scoffed, Jim, show me your soul, go on, get it out on your hand and show it to me! When he didn't answer, she said bitterly, It's your father, isn't it, and your mother. Pushing at you with all this stuff about your soul, they don't want a Proddy in their precious sainted family!

Because it was long past the moment when it would have been normal for Jim to say, How about we get married, Dolly? It was coming to her that he wasn't going to say anything like that. Not today, not tomorrow.

As far as she could see, being Catholic or Protestant wasn't such a big thing. Church was just what you did once a week. You said the prayers and you sang the hymns and then afterwards you stood outside the church having a good old gasbag. The C of Es like the Maunders stood outside their church and the RCs like the Murphys stood outside theirs, and then for the rest of the week you were just all in together. You bought your flour from their shop, you all went to school together, and it was only on Sundays that there was any difference that you could see.

But if a person was a Catholic it was the first thing you'd be told about them, as if it mattered. If a Protestant became a Catholic, people said they'd *turned*, like a traitor. And to marry a Catholic was a shocking thing, a mistake of nature.

It wasn't about the religion, Dolly thought. Your *eternal soul*. It was about being in a tribe. You were born into one tribe

39

or the other and you were supposed to stay there.

Poor Jim, he was in pain, he did love her. But not enough. Not enough to go against his family and the damn Pope somewhere talking Latin. He might love her, he could say the words and she could see it in his face, blotchy with feeling, but not enough to go against all that. So there was nothing in it.

Still, they kept on meeting. There was a hunger that was like a pain, a hunger you couldn't satisfy but you couldn't turn away from either.

The photographer came through town and everyone got their photos taken, and then Jim was asking her if she had one she'd give him. She brought it next time they met, a square no bigger than a postage stamp, her face looking out of it with a bit of a smile and her hair falling in a nice way.

Will you write on the back, Dolly, he said, and she looked at him, startled. Oh, now she understood. This was goodbye.

Was too proud to make a fuss, though, took the pen he handed her. He'd thought ahead, brought a pen! The special fountain pen he'd got for making his First Communion! Wrote on the back, she didn't have to think. *With love from Dolly.* There it was, she'd put herself on the line.

Go on, Jim, let's see what you're made of.

He held it cupped it in his palm for the longest time, as if to keep it safe, or secret. She thought he might have been trying not to cry. Then put it away carefully in his wallet, slid it into a little slot where no one would see.

Oh Jim, she thought. Why can't you have a bit of spine? Say bugger off to the whole kit and caboodle, the priests and the nuns and Jesus hanging from his cross, and that little dark box where you went in and told someone everything you'd done?

When they said goodbye that day, both of them knew it was the last time. The pony walked steadily along the boring old dusty road towards home and she was crying, though angry as much as sad. But in the middle of the tears she had a flash of understanding like a light shining out. You're weak, Jim Murphy, she thought. You won't put your money where your mouth is. The tears dried on her cheeks. She wasn't sad now, or angry. Just stony with what she knew about him.

And about herself: he was weak, but she was strong. She knew what she wanted and she was prepared to take it if she got a chance. She'd take a risk. She wasn't frightened, the way Jim was, of what people would say. Of what they'd think. Of some set of words that you believed because they came out of the Bible, when the Bible was just a lot of stories—told by men, mind—that had bugger-all to do with Dolly Maunder from Currabubula. What a swizz it was, what a swizz. Just to keep people down, keep them frightened like Jim was, and keep people like her from getting what they wanted.

After that Jim still made wistful eyes at her when they crossed paths in Curra, but she wanted to shout, Don't give me calf eyes, Jim Murphy, you had your chance and you threw it away!

The spot in the glade of trees was tainted from then on. She put her heels to Dash when they came up to it and she could feel his surprise, he'd got used to stopping there, but she hammered at his ribs and he broke into a trot. Got the idea quickly enough, the way she'd had to.

✤

Bert had become a flash young fellow. Had to have the best horse in the place, wouldn't get on anything else. Spent a lot of money on a good saddle and expensive boots.

And he'd turned out handsome. She had to hand it to him. That straight spine of a shearer, they learned not to bend their backs or they'd never last. Bert was straight and tall as a soldier, had a thick dark moustache, blue eyes with a bit of a triangular shape.

When he'd come to them at Forest Farm he'd been rough in his ways, showed the food in his mouth when he ate, picked up the bone to strip the last of the meat off it. But he'd learned as he went along and saw how other people did things. Now he could get every speck of meat off the bone with his knife and fork, neat as a surgeon.

He bought himself a cheap shiny watch chain even though he didn't have a watch. Saw her looking, saw the curl in her lip as he tucked the end of the chain into his vest pocket. You just wait, Dolly, he said with his flashing smile, and winked at her in that way he had, not worried that she didn't smile back. You just wait, that watch of mine's out there right this minute. Sitting on a bit of velvet in the shop waiting for me.

Smiling, unconcerned, unhurried. And he was right, he got the watch at last and then he was forever getting it out, just for the pleasure of clicking it open, feeling the gold in his palm.

Dolly's mother was always telling him how handsome he was, how tall, how strong. And oh, Bert love, your blue eyes! And then she'd glance at Dolly, to check if she was paying attention. Because she had her eye on Bert for her daughter. Dolly could see that. Keep him in the family, Dolly thought scornfully. So she could go on getting the bacon cured and sliced the way she liked. Her father too, he was in on it. He'd stitch that hard smile onto his face and say, Bert Russell, best man I ever had.

And Bert was looking Dolly's way. He'd twinkle at her, trying to make her laugh, or tempt her with the offer of a Sunday trip to Tamworth. Not that she wanted to go with him, but it was a way to get a change of scene. Have lunch at the Caledonian, the best pub in town, and sit in the lounge afterwards watching the graziers from the big spreads, the men in their pale cravats, the women fluttering along in silk frocks. He knew good spots for a picnic, too, out Goonoo Goonoo way or over to Duri. Sonny was always with them for appearances, he was courting his sweetheart Alma so they made up a little party. The men would have their guns and fire at a few targets or pick off rabbits. Dolly had a go and it turned out she was a good shot. Bert smiled that twinkly smile at her. My word, Dolly, a bloke'd better be careful around you!

Kid gloves. He kept Dolly in kid gloves. She thought it was pretty silly, just Bert Russell's idea of being up with the smart set, but she had to admit that it did feel good going to church in gloves. You felt like someone from some other kind of place than dusty little Currabubula.

43

He kept up the pressure. Made sure she heard when he said, My word Mrs Maunder, they'd have to go to the front parlour to get someone better than your daughter!

He was away fairly often, either at one of Dolly's father's other places or shearing on his own account. But even when he was away, he wasn't going to let her forget him. He had Wally, a wonderful horse, a real goer, Wally could go all day. Wherever he was, Bert would ride back of a Sunday, rain or shine, swinging off Wally and getting whatever it was he'd brought her out of the big pocket of his riding coat.

But she wasn't interested in Bert Russell. He was handsome, but not in a way that appealed to her. Partly it was because she remembered that dirty barefoot boy in the greasy-collared old coat at school, and the poor-person smell about him. Growing up like that with someone—it was like your brother, you didn't fancy them, even if they were good-looking.

So she was pert with him, never said thank you. Was happy to let him pay for lunch at the Cally, but when he tried to hold her hand she shook him off. He didn't seem to mind. She heard him talking to her father one day about a horse that he was haggling over. I'm a patient man, Mr Maunder, he said. Play the long game and you'll always win.

I know what you're up to, she thought. Yes, he might like her well enough, but it wasn't about her. It was about scrabbling his way up from that crooked little house by the creek. Tom Maunder would be giving his sons good spreads when they married. There'd be something for the right kind of son-in-law too.

Then there was a great scandal: Rose had to marry Ted Howlett. Dolly had known for a long time that Rose was walking out with Ted, but it had to be kept secret, because the Howletts were Catholics. She'd covered for Rose many times, done her work for her and been glad to do it. It was a way of pushing back against the thing that had come between her and Jim.

But Ted must have been bolder than Jim, because he and Rose were caught out. There was no gladness at Forest Farm, only Dolly's mother and father as silent and grim as if Rose was dead, not engaged to be married.

It wasn't so much that Ted and Rose had done the deed that made marriage necessary. In the world the Maunders lived in, it was no great shame if two young people in love couldn't wait for marriage. The shame was about the Catholic thing, having someone in your family join the other tribe.

And in her father's case there was something else as well. Dolly saw the way he couldn't look at Rose, wouldn't speak to her. His face was stiff with rage and disgust and maybe something like envy too, that someone had had that fun with his daughter.

The wedding was the first time Dolly had ever been in a Catholic church. It shocked her: not that it was different, but that it was the same. The same Bible, pretty much the same prayers, the same hard pews and the board floor where you could see the marks of the saw. Only the plaster saints and the

45

musty smell of the incense were different. All those lives made miserable, Jim lost to her, and for what?

Dolly watched her sister trying to make the best of things, smiling because a bride was supposed to smile, but showing one tooth too many to mean it. Ted was a good fellow, and a great hand with horses—he'd had a dream of going to Sydney to train them—but now he'd never have the chance to do more than what he was doing now, grubbing holes for other men's fences and ploughing other men's dirt. Dolly hadn't quite seen it before, the way the door closed on a person. You got that one chance, and you had to do the best you could with it.

Then, as if Rose had given them the idea, her brothers and sisters all got married, one after the other. Everyone was sure Sophia had missed the boat, she was over thirty, but Theo Durrant from Boggabri came along and took a fancy to her. Then Tom married Emma Parker and Eddie married Ada Ferrier.

When Tom married, Father gave him the place at Bellatta, and when Eddie married he got the one at Attunga. Dolly saw that it was a point of pride for a father to give his sons a place when they married. For daughters it was different. Father walked down the aisle with each one and when the reverend asked, Who giveth this woman? Father said, I do, and handed her over to the husband, the way you might hand over a parcel.

Once they'd all gone, the kitchen seemed very big. Now it was just Dolly and Sonny and Bert, and a girl called Beth from Nundle who'd come to help in the kitchen. Beth was a quiet little mouse of a thing, Dolly could hardly get a word out of her. Their voices echoed in the kitchen and the table seemed bare where all those others had been.

Minnie wrote to say she'd met a fellow called Arthur Innes. He had a good place near Dorrigo and she'd be getting married. Dolly read and re-read the letter. Of course she was pleased for Minnie. She sounded so happy and Arthur seemed a good fellow. But there was also a feet-out-from-under-you feeling. Her ally, the one who'd thought of the pupil-teaching, who'd laughed along with her at the girls doing boring old drawn-thread work for the tablecloths in their glory boxes, was gone. It felt like being abandoned, though of course it wasn't. What could a woman do but marry, and once you were married you belonged to your husband's world and had to turn your back on your own. It wasn't betrayal. It was the way the world was.

1909

Those Iron Rails

SHE was twenty-eight, not a girl any more. One of a kind now, the unmarried one. There was a feeling of people looking at her thinking, Well, you'd best get a move on, Dolly.

She knew what would happen to her if she didn't get married. She'd end up like Auntie Clara, still living with Granny Davis, her best years handed over to that old woman, day after dry old day out there on the verandah watching life go by. By the time Auntie Clara was free, it would be too late. She'd end up like Old Miss Trumper, a scurrying nervous little thing living with her brother's family, or Miss Henry, living on her own in a tumbledown place that was all that was left after the family farm got sold off. They were skinny shrivelled things now, hard to think they'd ever been young and juicy, but there'd have been a time when they had a man or two nosing about them. One way or another their moment had passed, the wave they might have ridden into marriage had broken and ebbed into a bit of foam and washed them up in a back street in Curra with nothing and no one. No, you had to get married. The trick was to get the right man, or at least the best you could get in the short time you had.

This wasn't some godforsaken place where girls were married off to the man her parents picked out. But in a way it was worse than those forced marriages, Dolly thought, because they're making out we're free to choose. All that flummery, the way a man's supposed to go down on one knee and beg, so the woman could say yes or no. It looked like choice, but it wasn't.

The cold reality was that marriage for most people she knew didn't have much to do with romance. It was a contract, the way Mr Murray had told them about Henry the Eighth and his wives. In Curra the contract was, if a woman wanted to have any kind of life she had to pick a man who could support her. Her side of the bargain was to keep house and do the necessary in bed. On the man's side, if he wanted to have a woman he had to earn money to support her. On both sides the whole business was pretty brutal. That was why people had to paper it over with the pretty pictures and the love stories.

Bert wasn't what she wanted, but there was this about him: she knew him. He was an easygoing-enough fellow. A hard worker. Not a drinker like a lot of men. And didn't have the blustery bullying way with women that so many men did, always putting you down.

Sharp as a tack, Bert said one day. My word, Dolly, you're sharp as a tack. She thought it sounded real, the admiration. He was no slouch himself, but didn't mind listening if a woman had a good idea.

He wasn't pretending to be in love, any more than she was. No calf eyes like Jim Murphy, no sighing and mooning over her photo. He was weighing up his choices, and so was she. With the door to being a married woman starting to creak shut, you took what you could get. She gave him the hint, he asked the question, she said yes. It was that simple to set your life on iron tracks into the future.

Her father had a big job on for Bert out on the Gunnedah place, so it was agreed that they wouldn't be getting married straightaway. That was fine by her. She could have a bit more time to be herself, Dolly Maunder, before she became Mrs Bert Russell. So when Minnie wrote from Dorrigo inviting Dolly to visit, she jumped at it.

Way off in the back corner of her mind, warming her with possibility, was a little flicker of hope. It wasn't anything she put into words, even to herself, but there was still a chance that some other door might spring open and show her another kind of future. Of course breaking an engagement was a scandalous thing, but it did happen. When it was the high-ups, it was called Breach of Promise. The lawyers got in on the act and a lot of money had to change hands. But between Dolly Maunder and Bert Russell it would be nothing more than gossip for a time. Then it would sink back below the surface of life in a sleepy village.

◆

Dorrigo was further than Dolly had ever travelled. First the train to Armidale, then Cobb's to the Dorrigo road, then a buggy from there to Minnie and Arthur's place. It was a foreign landscape, dense with forest, damp and lush, furrowed with steep gullies and ridges, everything interesting because it was different from home.

Minnie and Arthur lived outside the village in a neat weatherboard cottage that Arthur had built: he'd cut down the trees, sawn the planks, made every joint snug and true. He was a cheerful good-hearted fellow and you could see how he adored Minnie.

When he left the women to talk there was a little silence between them, as if they had to ease their way back to knowing each other. He made this table, Minnie said, and smoothed her hand gently over the grain as if it was skin. And the chairs.

She smiled, a proud wife. Dolly thought, We were the same once, Mr Murray used to say we were two peas in a pod. Now she's married, in that different world, and can we find a way to talk across the change that's come between us?

He's all right, Minnie said, and hesitated. Dolly could see she was wondering if she should say what she was thinking. That was sad, they'd never had secrets from each other.

Thing is, Minnie said, he'll go along with me. With what I

think about things. Told me, he reckons I'm the cat's whiskers in the brains department.

She laughed, and that laugh was the old Minnie.

That's true, right enough, she said. I've got more brains than him. But you know most men wouldn't say it. Look, it could be worse, Dolly, and that's the truth of the matter.

Dolly made herself smile, but Minnie knew her well enough to see there was no real gladness behind it.

We'll have a good time, Dolly, you and me, she said gently. Just like when we were girls together.

There was no going back, ever, to being girls together thinking they could be schoolteachers. But it was kind of her to pretend.

Of course Minnie knew about her and Bert, but Dolly wanted to have one last bit of being Dolly Maunder. Minnie didn't need to have it spelled out. It wouldn't be a secret, exactly, but no one needed to shout from the rooftops that Dolly Maunder was engaged to be married.

Dolly hadn't been at Dorrigo long when Minnie started to feel ill, pale in the face, shaky in the legs, rushing out to the privy to be sick every morning. It turned out there was nothing wrong, just that she was starting a baby. It was no lie for Dolly to send word home that Minnie needed her, she'd best stay another few weeks. Her mother agreed, a girl with morning sickness needed a good friend by her side.

Dolly was a little ashamed to have her mother think she was that *good friend*. If she was honest with herself, Minnie's morning sickness wasn't the whole truth. The real reason, the one that couldn't be spoken, could hardly even be admitted to herself, was Will Shaw.

Will Shaw was a friend of Minnie and Arthur's and was often over at their place. He was good-looking in a thin dark way. A bit of a dandy by Dorrigo standards: tied a kerchief round his neck, had a leather waistcoat with buttons made of farthings, wore his hair long at the back. Will was a bit arty, had a bit of a foreign feel, even though he was Dorrigo born and bred, his family timber-getters out Ferndale way. There was nothing arty or foreign about the Shaws.

But oh, he was a charmer, could play the piano and had a good singing voice, which it turned out Dolly did too, so he taught her a few songs and had her stand close beside him while his long fingers flickered away on the keys. Always picked her to be his partner at euchre, knocked his foot against hers under the table, and they had some kind of magic with the cards, won every time.

She hadn't known you could feel so alive, so enlarged, so full of fizz. It was quite a different thing from lying in the long grass with Jim Murphy. That had been about skins that wanted to be together, about a deep dangerous current in the blood that ran way below the surface of words. Certainly Dolly fancied the way Will Shaw looked, she liked that dandified thing about him, but this was about more than wanting to touch and be touched. This was about the person he was, and even more, it was about the sort of person she became when she was with him. As she'd become livelier, cleverer, wittier, with that man from the *Freeman*, with Will Shaw she became bigger, not squeezed down into something that was too small. She liked being that person.

Minnie saw which way the wind was blowing. When they were alone together one afternoon Dolly saw her casting around how to say what was on her mind.

Oh, our Will, she said, and watched Dolly. That Will Shaw!

Dolly worked to keep her face the same, but she knew Minnie wasn't fooled. Will Shaw, she said, trying to be light about it, yes, flash Will Shaw, eh.

But she couldn't look Minnie in the eye. Didn't know what to do with the feeling in her chest, when she said his name and thought about the person she was with him.

Got his head in the clouds, our Will, Minnie said. Dolly could hear her picking her way. The Shaws, they're all great men with an axe. Will's the joker in the pack.

Dolly knew what she was working her way around to and didn't want to hear it.

Work-shy, Minnie burst out with a big blurt of laughter. Arthur says Will's work-shy! Fact is, he's too smart for dear old Dorrigo.

Dolly heard the edge of emphasis in Minnie's voice. *Too smart for dear old Dorrigo.*

Wants to go to Sydney, see, Minnie said. Wants to write for the papers. Got his heart set on going to Sydney.

She didn't need to say the rest—*so he's not going to saddle himself with a wife.*

And now suddenly her mother was changing her tune,

wanted Dolly back straightaway. But she delayed and delayed. There was always an excuse. The creek was up. There was a bushranger about. The wheel on the buggy was broken. Her mother's tone got harder with every letter and finally she wrote to say, *If you're not back here by next week, your father says he'll come and get you.* The thought of her father—black with anger, making the long trip to haul her home, wasting all that time when he could have been working—made her write back that she was on her way.

There were no tears as she sat in Arthur's buggy to get to the Armidale road, none when Cobb's coach came jolting along and she kissed Minnie goodbye, none as she sat in the train on the undeviating iron rails that would take her down to Currabubula. Nothing as soft as tears, just a bitter coldness at her heart.

Tom Connolly could pick whatever woman he and his family wanted. Jim Murphy could warm himself at the little cosiness of his forbidden love. Will Shaw could go off to Sydney, strike up conversations with men in pubs until one of them gave him a job writing for the papers.

A woman couldn't do any of that. Couldn't take her future in her own hands and shape it the way she wanted. Couldn't even be a teacher if she wanted, and that was surely a humble enough thing to wish for.

There'd been a big send-off for Will the week before. He'd kissed her hand like some old gallant and made everyone laugh, and done that right-into-the-eyes thing he did, so you felt you were the only other person in the world. Then he was gone.

Dolly knew he'd never think about her again, Dolly Maunder who he'd showed off for, winking at her over his cards and singing to her with his fine voice. She wouldn't even be a memory for him, she knew, once he got to that new life in Sydney, his real life, the one he was made for.

For her there was nothing to do but get in the buggy and start the long journey into her future as Mrs Albert Russell.

Mr and Mrs Russell were married in January 1910. Her mother's eyes were glistening, saying goodbye to her and Bert at the station afterwards. Dolly watched her go up on tiptoes to kiss Bert on the cheek and thought, Yes, that's why I had to marry him, you wanted that ghost back, that ghost of Willie.

Rose was there, watching her little sister trying not to think about what lay ahead of her. They'd never been much for hugging, they weren't a hugging family, but now Rose hugged Dolly hard. Dolly felt her big breasts against her own bony chest, smelled the comfortable human smell of a hardworking woman, felt Rose's breath hot in her ear.

You'll be right, Rose said, you'll be right, Dolly dearest.

In this moment of saying goodbye they were the closest they'd ever been, and that unlocked something in Dolly, not tears so much as a hard choking in her throat and her chest, but could you cry from helpless rage? The only word she could think of, the word that came up in every direction her mind went, was No! No! No!

Standing there at the station she could feel everything dropping away, all the threads that bound her to who she was, to her aunts and uncles and cousins, and beyond family, to everyone else in Currabubula, all those people who'd known her since she was a baby. There was the Davis Hotel behind her, where Grandfather Davis had put his thing into old Granny Davis's thing all those years ago and started her mother's life. Now, all these years later, here was that woman's daughter standing with her little cardboard suitcase, her hat trying to blow off and her dress pressing against her legs in a gust of wind, a person taking the step that would push her out into the unknown.

They spent their honeymoon at the Caledonian Hotel in Tamworth. That was Bert's idea. Nothing but the best, the best hotel in town and the best room, the Honeymoon Chamber. Dolly had never slept in such a big airy room, or in such a grand bed—with a canopy! There were beautiful cedar chests of drawers for your clothes, and a carpet so plush it was like walking on velvet.

We'll get some photos done, Dolly, Bert said. Put our glad rags on again. I've booked us in at Fletcher's.

Oh no, Bert, Dolly said, we don't need any photos!

She couldn't say why she didn't want photos, but she didn't. The wedding was over. No need to go back to it.

But Bert laughed. Oh come on Dolly, he said. You only get married once!

That stopped her. *You only get married once.* He said it so lightly, just a throwaway line, but it was a reminder of the rope round her neck.

Bert got her a new bouquet, she did her hair with the combs and pins again, got back into the wedding dress. The dress smelled sour, already something from the past. The wedding day had disappeared in a flurry, the shouting and awkward speechifying and everyone laughing and joshing and the champagne like hot fingers in her chest. It had been a matter of putting one foot after the other. But after two days of being a married woman, she truly understood that this would be the rest of her life. Now, in this hot photographer's studio, a dead stony thing sat where the flurry had been.

Smile, dear, Mr Fletcher shouted, lovely smile now Mrs Russell! She tried, she even thought she'd managed some kind of smile while he went under the camera and the stuff blazed out sudden in the dish.

Well, she might have thought she was smiling, but when they got the pictures back there it was for all the world to see: the downturned mouth, the eyes pinched up with secret crying, and her fist gripping the bouquet like a cudgel.

1910

Mrs Russell of Rothesay

GUNNEDAH was fifty miles from Currabubula, out on the blacksoil plains to the north-west, and Rothesay—Dolly's father's place—was another five miles west of the town. He'd known what to look for. Rothesay was on a prime bit of country. You could run sheep or cattle, but the big money was in wheat.

Dolly's father wasn't giving the place to Bert and Dolly straight out. The idea was, they'd work the place as share-farmers for a few years, save enough to buy it.

The first morning there she stood on the verandah looking down over the paddocks where the wheat was bending and shifting under a warm breeze. She couldn't believe how a day's journey from Curra had brought her to what might as well have been a different continent. Out here there were no enfolding hills as there were at home. This was a landscape of height and air and space. There was that vast bowl of sky above her and a sense of being able, just about, to see the curve of the earth as it turned through space. You were closer to the sky, right up inside it, and that gave you a weightless feeling that there was nothing to hold you down, you might float away. A different air, too: not the dusty dry of Forest Farm but a clear crisp thin-aired kind of dry that made you want to snuff up great nosefuls of it. The house sat in the middle of the flatness, so from every window the eye could travel, without obstacle, all the way to the soft place where the horizon became the sky.

Until now, as she looked out over the gleaming endless land with its moving skin of wheat, she'd never realised just how closed-in, how narrow, how hemmed-in, things were at Curra, that village squeezed into the kink in the range. When you were in Curra there were just two ways to go, down the kink to the south or up the kink to the north, and every single thing was familiar and old and stale. Whereas out here, whichever way you looked, the endless space was like an invitation.

The track to Gunnedah—a wide flat open town on that wide flat open plain—ran past the front door. It would be a new beginning there. She wouldn't be Dolly Maunder, known to everyone since before she was born, everything about her already judged. She'd be Dolly Russell from out at Rothesay, a brand-new person in the world who could make her own choices about who she was.

Mistress of her own domain. Must be a line from some poem, wouldn't Mr Murray be pleased she remembered it. But that was what she was. Starting now: her place, her life. No mother, no father, to tell her what to do or put obstacles in her path. Only her husband, but she'd be able to manage him. He wasn't the one she'd wanted, but just think if she'd somehow got that Tom Connolly from Murrurundi, or dear old Jim Murphy. She'd be hung about with a whole lot of in-laws and busybody relatives coming and going and peering and tutting and saying how they'd done things in their day. Here it was just her and Bert and the sky.

➦

Bert got up early every morning. She'd pretend to be asleep as he padded out to the kitchen in his socks. She'd hear him lighting the fire, filling up the kettle. He was a man of habit, she knew the next sound would be the rattle of the bread box and the little knocking from where he was cutting the bread on the warped board. The tea caddy, open and shut. The cup tinkling on its saucer.

She'd known him all her life, just about, so there hadn't been too many surprises after they married. Knew the way he pursed his lips towards his glass of beer, the way he smoothed his thick moustache after every swallow of it, the way he put his muscled hand down beside the plate when he'd finished his dinner. What he liked in the middle of the day: a cold chop and a hunk of strong cheese. What he liked after tea: bread and jam. What he liked in bed: well, it wasn't too bad. He knew to sweet-talk her first. You're a pretty thing, Dolly Russell, he whispered, and she didn't say, How can you tell, Bert, it's dark. The surprise was that the thing wasn't bad at all, not like some women made out.

She'd always known that his bluff cheerful manner was a way of keeping himself private. You'd never know what he was feeling. He never lost his temper, never shouted, never swore. He'd smile but not really answer if you asked him something outright, and on the rare occasions a letter came for him, he'd slip it in his pocket to read later. Married to him, she was coming to understand just how contained and locked-up he was, even in the way he dressed, his trousers cut high around his waist and nipped in, his bootlaces pulled tight as a corset.

She'd watch him sideways as they sat by the fire of an evening. Would you ever know what he was thinking? As it was for her father, she thought, a measure of strength was to be secretive, to give no one the power of knowing what kinds of emotions beat around in his chest. From that muddled, poverty-racked home, he'd come out a man who liked things orderly, neat, everything packed away out of sight. And from that shameful home came the secretiveness too, she supposed. Wanting to leave his beginnings behind.

She still didn't know the ins and out of the story about his mother, though the outline was obvious enough. She'd asked him once or twice, but he wouldn't say. Oh, no need to go over all that now, he'd say, and if she asked again, he'd leave the room and clatter about in the kitchen.

He didn't keep in touch with all his brothers and sisters,

only the two close to him in age, the ones Dolly remembered from school. Arthur was doing well in Sydney, he was a bookie. Or maybe just a bookie's runner, he might have been gilding the lily in his letters. Allan, the younger one, had a farm somewhere and was doing all right. Henry Newitt had taken Mary and the other children and gone to Queensland, apparently, that much Bert told her. He couldn't be made to say anything else.

I never look back, he said. If he had a creed to live by, it was that: *I never look back*.

◆

The wheat started well the first year, but as the season went on there wasn't enough rain for a decent crop. That was what you had to expect out here. It was good country but you couldn't count on rain, not every year. Disappointing, but not the end of the world because Bert could get ready money working on other people's places. Shearing, fencing, ploughing, he'd turn his hand to anything. He'd be home again a few weeks later, stay for a month or six weeks and do everything that needed doing around the place, then he'd be off again.

She knew all the locals now, all the wives, did her bit for the church fete, even put a cake in the Gunnedah Show just to be in the swim with the other women. She wasn't going to try the marmalade, there was bad blood there. Mrs Ellis wanted to win, wanted it so badly she told Dolly, in the strictest confidence, that just before it set she'd arrange the shreds of peel with a pair of long-handled tweezers so they were scattered perfectly up and down the jar. But what Mrs Ellis didn't know, which Dolly learned from old Hank Pickup, was that, no matter how good her marmalade was, Mrs Ellis would never win, because Mrs White had an in with the judges.

Dolly woke up every morning thinking of a project and it fuelled her all day. Small things: she'd plant pansies in that old waggon wheel lying in the grass, she'd seen it done at Aunt Emma's at Bendemeer and she'd never forgotten. Big things: going over to the new kinds of wheat they were bringing out, that didn't get the rust. No matter what you were doing, there was always a better way to do it.

Whereas Bert was inclined to accept whatever came along. Oh well, we *could*, he'd say, when she told him about the waggon wheel or the new kind of wheat. It wasn't that he was lazy, though when she got cranky she accused him of that. The real reason was that he didn't like change. He plodded along, working hard, his horizon small, his ambitions modest, sticking to the familiar, not taking any risks.

But she'd get an idea in her head and it wouldn't leave her. She'd keep at him and keep at him.

By God, Dolly, he said one day, resigned but admiring as well, you never give up, do you.

✦

Bert was away on a shearing job when Jim Murphy turned up one day, just turned up at the kitchen door. What a quiet

66

place it was, suddenly, with Jim standing in her kitchen smiling his easy smile. No one about, the closest would have been the Donohues over at Fairview. He had some story about a cousin with a place along the river.

Just happened to be in the district? she said, and he smiled back.

That's right, Dolly, just happened to be in the district.

Seeing him drinking tea in her kitchen, in the chair that Bert always sat in, Dolly knew Jim Murphy was under her skin in some way that Bert never was and never would be, for all that she and Bert knew every wrinkle of each other, where she and Jim had always had those layers of fabric between them. It wasn't something you could choose. It went deeper than picking one man over another. And it wasn't something you could go against. Not for long.

To begin with it was chitchat about the folk in Curra, and then it was showing him round. At the door of the bedroom they glanced in at the white counterpane covering the bed. Looked at it and then away. They wouldn't be going in there.

They did it on the floor, on the thick wool rug in the main room. They didn't talk about what they were doing but she could see written on Jim's dear face the same thing she knew was on hers: something ecstatic but blank, as if you—the person you were in the world—had slipped out of the room and left your body behind to go on without you. She didn't ask him what had made him change his mind. Didn't ask about that eternal soul of his. Whatever his answer, it was too late.

It wasn't just the one visit. But Jim must have had an ear

to the ground about where Bert was, because when Bert was home Jim kept away.

Later she worked out the dates, sitting at the kitchen table with the calendar from Gunnedah Meats in front of her, a crow walking on the tin roof over her head, and she laughed, a hard laugh like a cry of pain. This baby that was taking shape inside her must have started at the end of March or the beginning of April. Jim had visited around then. She couldn't know, not for certain. What if it was written on the child's face for all to read, what she'd been up to?

Whichever way it turned out, she knew it was the end of things with Jim. He'd do the dates too and, poor silly man, he'd take the easy road. He'd stay away.

✤

Frank was a big baby and he took a long time to force his way out. Ripped her down there, she felt the sharp cold pain like a blade. Mrs Lynch went on saying what it seemed she'd been saying for days, You're doing real good Mrs Russell, real good, big breath Mrs Russell, push now dear, push for all you're worth.

He came out at last all of a whoosh, she felt warm liquid everywhere, and a relief like getting out the most almighty stool, and the thought was so funny that she laughed, a deep laugh that shook the bed. Mrs Lynch had seen everything and heard everything. She smiled and said, You done real good Mrs Russell, here's your bonny boy, and there he was, a solid bundle in her arms and a great head of dark hair slicked down flat on his head, and his eyes looking at her as if he knew her from long ago, and he was Bert, Bert to the very life.

It was touching to see Bert go soft with him, cradling that little head in his enormous hands and making soft clucking noises to stop him crying. My black sheep, he'd say, fluffing up Frank's head of dark curly hair, and Dolly watched him so deft and soft with the baby, and thought, I could have done a lot worse.

One afternoon when Frank was a few months old, she left him asleep and—to get out of the house for a few minutes— went into the garden. Bert was away again and the days could seem endless, just her and the baby. She wandered into the shed, there was something about the quality of the silence there that she liked, different from the airy silence outside, and it was peaceful, with fingers of bright sunlight streaming down through the holes in the tin roof and dust dancing in those beams of yellow brilliance.

She was sitting on the old trunk there when the dog wandered in. She flicked its silky ears back and forth, stroked under its chin when it ducked its head to sniff at the padlock on the trunk.

She wondered later what would have happened if Ikey hadn't wandered into the shed at that moment, if he hadn't ducked his head and sniffed at the padlock. Because why a padlock? At Rothesay nothing needed locking up.

It was the work of a moment to get the crowbar from where it hung with the other tools. She wasn't thinking what or why, was in a kind of trance of idle curiosity. It didn't take much for the old rivets to loosen and the whole thing come away, padlock and all. There was a brown cardboard box, and inside the box there was a pile of papers, and because Bert was a tidy man it took her no time to see what they were about.

Which was: payments to Elizabeth Jane Burgess for the support of her daughter Mary Anne, born on the 15th of July 1909, to be continued until said Mary Anne shall attain the age of sixteen years, signed Albert James Russell, and there was Bert's big showy signature on every page.

It didn't make any sense, who was Elizabeth Jane Burgess and who was this Mary Anne, and what was Bert's signature doing sprawled on every page? She stared at the paper, the printed parts and the handwritten parts, and then in a flare of understanding she knew.

Little mousy Beth, always in the corner of the kitchen at Forest Farm. Dolly had gone away to Dorrigo, and stayed and stayed, mooning over Will Shaw, and Bert had got busy with Beth. She'd had this daughter, and Bert was paying for her support.

At first it was amazement, that Bert had a secret from her. She was the one with the lie running along under every day. Then she looked again at the date. She and Bert had stood up in front of the minister in the January of 1910. Bert had written his name all over these papers the August before, when this Mary Anne was a month old. It was soon after that, the September, that Dolly had come back from Dorrigo. She hadn't given much thought to Beth being gone. Oh, she went to

Queensland somewhere, her mother had said, and Dolly hadn't given little Beth another thought.

She looked at the papers again. There was her mother's name, right under Bert's signature, *Witness: Sarah Catherine Maunder.* Her mother had known! Known, and still chivvied away at her to marry Bert!

In fact—her mind running quick as a mouse—it must have been her mother who organised these support payments. Bert wouldn't have known how to go about it. Her mother, getting rid of the little miss in the pantry and rushing Dolly back from Dorrigo quick sticks, before Bert could have second thoughts.

Her father must have known too. Walking down the aisle giving her away, he'd have been thinking, My word, that was a near thing. Sonny would have known. And how many others? There must be people who'd smiled at the wedding— Oh, congratulations, Dolly!—who all the time were laughing behind their hands. Poor old Dolly, she doesn't know.

Oh, it was burning blood in the face, of hot rage. And it was a falling feeling too, a feeling of having lost herself. She'd been so pleased with her own cleverness, thought she was making a cool canny decision in marrying Bert. While all the time she was being steered along, the way you prodded a pig into a pen. Now there was a gaping hollow where her sense of herself had been.

Back in the house, picking up Frank and putting him to the breast, there was another thought that cut her like a blade. Frank was her first child, but he wasn't Bert's first. She'd gone all soft, watching him cradle the child's head, and she'd thought they shared that first-time wonder. But had he cradled that other baby the same way, just for that month or so before Beth went away? Even the unexpected pleasure of sharing that delight with Bert was poisoned, ruined, one more thing to mock her.

As she sat by the fire after tea, listening to the wind in the big pines, all those miles that it had travelled before it got tangled in the dark branches and made its eerie song, the whole story went around and around in her mind. That girl. She'd given her a bit of lace once, nothing much, a little collar, not new, it was a gift from Aunt Em but Dolly had never liked it. She'd wondered at the odd look the girl gave her as she took the scrap of stuff. The girl must have been busy with Bert even then. That look was embarrassment, confusion, wanting to be grateful to Dolly, but laughing at her too. Poor silly Dolly, thinking she was being Lady Bountiful.

That was the unspeakable, unbearable thing. The humiliation.

✢

She thought of all the ways she was going to give Bert hell when he got back and she let fly as soon as he was in the door. But she'd hardly got into her stride when he fired back. What about that bloody Jim Murphy nosing round here like a dog after its vomit? Oh yes Dolly, don't think I didn't know.

How did he know? But of course, too late she realised there were no secrets in a little place like this. It was no different from Curra. Any movement along the quiet dust of the road would be marked, any unknown horse noticed, let alone an unknown man. The country might look empty, but there was always someone watching.

Still, she came straight back at him. Oh, I might as well, she shouted, heard her voice crack. Might as well have had a bit of fun with Jim, the way you did with that girl.

She was in the wrong, of course. But then so was he. She was hurt, and she was guilty too, and how did you sort out a muddle like that?

I'm not going to put up with it, she shouted. She didn't know what she meant but it felt good saying it, the muddle clearing into the lovely clean simple thing of anger. Grabbed the saucepan, banged away with it on the stove, bang bang bang, felt the shock up her arm, a kind of ecstasy of hard noise. You can go, Bert, you can just bloody go.

And now he was standing up, tall in the low kitchen. Too right I will, Dolly, he said, that grim quiet. I've had enough.

He left the next day after a night on the divan. She stood in the kitchen watching him strap up his kitbag.

I'm off now, Dolly, he said without looking at her, and he might have meant he was going to the crutching job over at Manilla or he was leaving for good. She didn't know, couldn't think, and Frank was crying, and when she tried to look at what was happening, it was just a big blur like some bit of arithmetic that Mr Murray might have given them, full of pluses and minuses and things in brackets and things divided and things multiplied. You had to get your mind very steady to

73

work out how to go about it and her mind was not steady, not steady at all. She watched Bert go, the horse's tail twitching, and him leaning down to undo the gate, and she remembered Willie. At least he didn't have to go through anything like this.

The wound-up feelings kept her going for a few days. She was warmed, too, by the thought that she might write to Jim. Dear Jim. She made a little picture out of it: Jim across the table from her, smiling, taking her hand, the two of them living their lives together, the way they always should have. Oh, it'd be a scandal for a time. But they wouldn't care, and once everyone knew, and had their fill of saying wasn't it disgraceful, the heat would go out of it. Something else would soon come along for them to be shocked about.

But by the time she'd got the paper and pen out of the dresser drawer she knew there was nothing to write. Jim hadn't taken her when he could have had her fair and square. If he wouldn't risk his eternal soul by marrying her, he was never going to live with her without being married, and with a baby that wasn't his as well.

The place was awfully silent. She sat at the kitchen table, watching the steam curl out of the spout of the kettle, Frank in his crib near the stove. *She couldn't keep him, you know*, that was what they said about women whose husbands deserted them. No matter who'd done what, it was always the woman's fault.

She went over the bleak landscape of her choices. She couldn't run the farm on her own: harness up the horses, bring in the wheat. There was no money to pay men to do it. Her brothers might help out now and then, but they had their own

74

wives and children to look after. The only reason the place was a going concern was that Bert brought in that ready money from shearing.

If it wasn't for Frank she could try going it alone, house-maid in a hotel, taking in laundry, something of that kind. But not with a little baby. And down the end of that path was Bert's mother, that woman with eight children by who knows how many men and a great stink of shame hanging over her.

Or she could trail back to Forest Farm, beholden to her father for every mouthful, hating her mother for having deceived her. Oh, if only her father had let her go school-teaching, there might be some kind of life to be made now. If he'd said yes. Or if she'd insisted. Could she have gone on a hunger strike like those suffragette women?

Well, she hadn't. No one had helped her and she hadn't been strong enough.

Frank cried, he'd become a fretful baby, as if, little bub that he was, he could feel all her hurt and helpless rage. Arched his back away from the breast, kicking his feet, turning his head aside as if her milk had turned bitter. No wonder, all those sleepless nights thinking, How dare he, how dare my mother, but the panic too. What am I going to do?

There was only one way forward. She might pretend to herself, but at last she had to recognise what she'd known from the beginning: no matter how bad a marriage was, it had to be endured.

Old Billy O'Brien came through on his way to the Manilla shed, cadged a cup of tea and a meal. She gave him a note for

Bert, safe enough since Billy couldn't read even his own name. A few days later she was on the verandah and saw the little puff of dust in the distance that meant a man on a horse was coming. She had those few minutes, until she could see the man was Bert, to sit on her feelings the way she'd sat on that bloody trunk, pressing them down. She watched him swing off his horse, glance at her then away, as if she was too bright to look at.

How's Frank getting along, he said, fiddling with his pack at the back of the saddle. Going all right, is he.

They weren't questions, any more than whatever she said was an answer. It was just a way of saying, There's no point going back over anything. We've got what we've got, and that's all there is to it.

＊

She thought about her mother, all the ways she'd like to hurt her. Scribbled a little note full of how dare you, how could you. But even as she was writing it she knew there were no words that would punish her mother. No words that could turn the pain back, so that her mother had to suffer it the way Dolly did. No words that could change the bitter hurt that she woke up with every day and went to bed with every night.

The only thing was to get away. Away from the farm her father owned, which would still feel like his even if they ever made enough to buy it. Away from Gunnedah, where the Maunders were part of the broad web of country connections. Away far enough that her mother would be cut off: from Bert, who she'd wanted so much that she'd wronged her own daughter, and cut off too from her baby grandson, and any other children that might come along.

It couldn't happen overnight. She couldn't hope for that. But she and Bert would get the money together to find a farm somewhere else, way down south or up in Queensland. In the meantime she'd make sure she found one reason after another not to see her father and mother, and as soon as the chance came to get away, she'd seize it.

✦

She was getting into the habit of being a nag, she knew. She heard her voice going shrill, rousing on Bert for all the small things, when what drove her to madness was the one big thing. No matter how much she railed and ranted at him, there was no putting that right.

He made good money and gave it to her, all but the money for that girl. He cut the wood and carried the water. He took Frank out with him when he could, took him out ploughing at times. She asked him once, What do you do when Frank's sleepy? Oh, he said, I lie him down in a furrow, put my coat round him, he's snug as a bug.

He never asked if Frank was his. But the warmth he and Dolly had shared, back in those first days, was gone. Making their marriage work was the next thing to be done, and he put his hand to it as he'd put his hand to everything else. It was of a piece with that boy she'd known twenty years before, going at Ted Abbott with no passion, as if teaching Ted Abbott to keep his mouth shut about his mother was nothing more than a job of work to be done. Making some kind of a life with Dolly was the job at hand now, and he'd get on and do that.

Counting the weeks later, she realised it might have been the night of Bert's return, December 1911, that the new baby was started. Nance was born so close to Frank that it felt sometimes as if they were twins. But she was a more difficult baby than Frank. Dolly would go round and round the things that she might be crying about: was her nappy wet? Was she hungry, was she tired? But still the child would cry till Dolly couldn't stop herself shouting, What's the matter? What's the bloody matter? And of course Nance would cry harder. Then Frank would start grizzling, so both their little faces were ugly with unhappiness.

Dolly felt boxed in, helpless, frantic to unchain herself from their wanting, wanting, wanting. Even when they were peaceful she found it hard to be gentle with them. She heard her voice sharp, knew her movements impatient as she dressed them and fed them. It was as if the pain in her heart had got into them both and made them mirrors to her own misery. She looked at them sometimes with a stony feeling. It wasn't their fault, but they were part of her humiliation. Frank had been the most tender part of her life, and Nance should have been another. Now there was something hard, like a slab of scar, where softness for them should have been.

Even Bert, usually so patient, lost his temper with Nance

one night. Picked her up from the crib where Dolly had put her—almost thrown her, if truth be told—picked up the red-faced bundle squalling at exactly the pitch to set your teeth on edge, and carried her outside. Dolly stood at the door, watching, the night cold, the stars small in the black sky. Bert leaned over the horse trough, tipped the child down, dunking her head. Dolly could hear the splutter and splash, and had a moment of crimson satisfaction. There! See! That's what you get! Bert lifted the child out and the cry started again, a different note, worse, harder to bear. Put her back in, Dolly thought. Right under, till she stops.

A terrible thought, she crushed it back down into wherever it had come from. Took a step towards them. She heard her voice a thin quaver: Bert? And there was Bert, carrying the child under his arm like a log of wood, pushing the wet bundle at her, going inside without looking back, and Dolly knew he'd had the same thought.

After that they were both ashamed, and quiet with the child. But cool towards her too. Nance had uncovered something deep and violent and ugly in both of them, brought it out into the air. It was hard to forgive her for that.

◆

When the war started, Dolly got in the habit of buying the newspaper whenever she went in to Gunnedah. The papers were full of how awful the Germans were—bayoneting babies! There were hints of even worse things but they never came out and said it. Dolly was somehow drawn to the horrors, as if some dark violent thing in herself was being played out in those smudged inky little paragraphs. Of course it was shocking what the Germans were doing but as you read it you felt a kind of excitement. She wasn't the only one. In town, the other wives told each other what they'd all read, handing monstrous things to each other backwards and forwards as if to feel again that kick of outrage. Is it that we're dead inside, she thought, that we're so drawn to that little pulse of feeling?

All around them the farms were emptying of young men. People's sons and brothers and husbands were going off to enlist, mothers and sisters and wives with their hankies at their eyes at the railway station, and always some older man shouting out, Hip hip hooray for our brave boys! *Brave boys* was all very well, and that was all the papers talked about, but Dolly knew plenty of them were doing it for the six shillings a day and the chance of a few adventures.

Bert didn't pore over the papers the way she did and she could see he never for a moment thought of enlisting. Not that he was a coward. But he'd never been one for grand words and flag-waving, any more than she was. King and Country had never done anything for the Russells or the Maunders, only the sweat of their own brows. He chipped in with the other men to get the harvest in and the shearing done on the places where the men were off fighting, and he bought the war bonds. But like the other men with farms and families, he knew a man couldn't just go off. How would a woman with little children manage, on a farm a mile from the nearest neighbour? Besides, an army marches on its stomach and someone had to stay home and grow the wheat. The papers were full of how women were handing out white feathers, but that was in the cities. There was none of that nonsense in the country.

Her pleasure in the pieces in the paper came from the certainty that none of it had anything to do with her. Germans were just something to frighten the children with when they were playing up. But when the telegrams with black edges started arriving at farms around the place, and you started to see men with missing arms or legs on the streets of Gunnedah, it became real. Then she couldn't stomach the newspapers. She hung onto Bert in the night. She was glad he was no coward, but no fool patriot either.

◆

Three years after Nance was born, Max came along. Frank and Nance were wound up like little springs, but Max was a different kind of person entirely, as if something combative between his parents had burned out by the time he came along. A sunny smiling peaceful babe, happy to lie and look.

Dolly knew you were supposed to love all your children the same, but if truth were told she loved Max in a way she couldn't quite love the children of that miserable time. As Frank and Nance got older she made an effort to be soft with them, but they sensed how she had to work at it, and that made it worse. But when Max looked up at Dolly and his face blossomed into a smile, some tight-wound feeling in her melted. At last, a child free of the darkness, a child born into a house where, if not peace, there was at least a truce.

A crust seemed to have grown over the bitterness now. She hardly ever saw her parents, the war made a good excuse. As for Bert, he and she had got into some kind of jogtrot together. He was still paying that girl, she knew, though he never gave a sign of thinking about her or the baby they'd made. She tried to forget that shadow family tracking along beside her own. She resented the money, but at the same time had to pity Beth. Imagine being out there in the cold world, alone except for a helpless child. It was the story of Bert's mother, of course. No woman could wish that on another.

But the hurt of it was the great stinging wound in her life. When a small thing cracked open the crust, and the bitterness bubbled up and she let fly, she'd watch Bert's mouth harden. He'd say nothing, just smooth his moustache, clear his throat, and leave her to swallow the feelings again.

1918

The Rivers of Africa,
the Mountains of Europe

JUST across the river from Rothesay was Malcolm Mackellar's spread, Kurrumbede. The Mackellars were old squatting money and had the best place on the Namoi as well as a big house beside the harbour in Sydney. Malcolm's sister Dorothea lived there but came up to Kurrumbede now and then, and Dolly sometimes saw her in town. No one in Gunnedah had shoes like Dorothea's, dainty slim shoes with buttons up the side. You'd have to have a maid to do up all those tiny buttons. Bourne's Store got hold of one of her poems that had been published, stuck it up in a frame in the window as if this city silvertail had given them their gospel to live by. *I love a sunburnt country, a land of sweeping plains, of ragged mountain ranges, of drought and flooding rains.*

Well, Dolly thought, it was all very well for her. She could go back to Potts Point when the going got hard. It was different for her and Bert when there was a bad drought and the crops shrivelled away in front of your eyes, or the rain came and flooded you out.

The sky could be your enemy, blank and blue day after weary hot day when it was dry. There was nothing to love about that sunburnt country then. Nothing to love about flooding rains either, when it was a matter of the endless water coming down out of the dark sky, streaming brown over your paddocks, plucking your hard-hacked fences out of the ground and pushing at the hayshed till it fell over, the precious hay floating away to nowhere, and when the water went down again, nothing left but sticky black mud and another year without a crop.

Your whole life came down to the whim of the weather, the sky a mocking tyrant. The worst of it was the not-knowing, the way you could never make a plan. No wonder people used to make sacrifices, she thought, a goat or their first-born or whatever. At church when there was a drought on, the minister always prayed for rain, and Dolly bowed her head with the rest but thought, God's not listening to Mr Peters.

Every year Bert ploughed and sowed. Dolly could stand on the verandah and see the shimmer of green that meant the wheat had sprouted. There was always hope. Have a bumper crop, make enough to get away. But for six years that hopeful green came to nothing. It was no rain, or too much rain. Or it was the grasshoppers, or the sooty mould, or the mice. As one year, two years, three years went by without a crop, she told herself not to hope. But what else could you do, stuck there under the bowl of sky, but plant the damn wheat and hope?

The seventh year, 1917, they were sure it would be a good crop at last, the stalks bending over with the weight of the full ears of grain, heavy with plenty. The men were coming to help with the harvest the next day.

The morning started fine, but as the afternoon came on something peculiar started to happen on the horizon. A great tangled tube of cloud came towards them, coiling over itself as it moved across the sky, seething against a background of smeared grey. The air was suddenly full of huge wind, leaves and sticks violently hurled up, rattling against the windows. Dolly watched a shrivelled hole in the cloud opening slyly around a ragged edge of smear, and a line of lightning like a crack in fine china, white and sharp against the dark cloud. And the boiling tube of cloud plaiting itself into itself as it rolled slowly across the sky, so dark a grey it was almost blue, shot with that cold white lightning.

There was nothing to say. Nothing to be done to fight the evil coiling thing coming towards them. They could see the wall of rain advancing over the paddocks, could watch it engulf the big tree that stood alone on the boundary. It was roaring as it came, and sending cold air at them, dank and dangerous. Then it was on top of them, not rain but hail, lumps like fists, the sky punching and punching at them, hurling the hail at the ground so violently that it bounced up and made a seething cloud along the ground.

It lasted five minutes. Stopped suddenly, a strange strained silence after the din, the air clearing to show them what it had done: every single blade of wheat, a year's work and hope, flattened and pummelled into a tangled mess of mud and straw.

We're going, Dolly told Bert that night. She'd started off shouting but now she was calm. We're not going to stay here, Bert. We're going. He looked at her, his smooth face that hid whatever he was thinking. Oh, he said, and where have you got in mind, Dolly?

He was being nasty, of course, what could she have in mind, where could they go? But as her little flame of rage leapt up to meet his scorn she saw exactly what she had in mind: a little shop, far away from Gunnedah and Currabubula and that cruel sky. The picture of it came to her so clearly she knew it must have been there, hidden in her thoughts, for years. She'd never thought beyond another farm and she'd thought they'd need a windfall, that bumper crop they hoped for every year. That had never happened, but it turned out that disaster could do the same job.

It would be like Lewes' shop in Curra—she could still remember going in there and looking around at so much plenty in so many sacks and boxes and barrels. Everything was weighed out by hand, so all the smells mingled, bacon, raisins, sugar, cheese, biscuits. Everyone needed all those things. And in a shop it didn't matter what the weather was doing.

We'll write to your brother Arthur, she said. He can find

us a little shop somewhere down Sydney way. He'll know how to go about it. Touch him for a stake to get started, he's always telling us how well he's doing.

Bert watched as she laid it out. He might think she was making it up on the fly, but as the words came out it all made sense. And she could see he was tempted.

It was a big leap. She didn't know anyone who'd made a leap that big. Her father hadn't had that kind of choice, because all he knew was how to plough and how to shear. Rose didn't either, or Tom or Sophia, because to make the leap off a farm you had to know things that only schooling could give you. She and Bert had been taught how to write a business letter, work out an account, do an order, make an invoice. And although it had seemed silly to learn about those places they'd never see—the Rivers of Africa, the Mountains of Europe—at least learning about them told them there was more to the world than the little bit of country that was all they knew. There was a bigger world, and you could have bigger ideas.

Bert was quiet for a long time. She let him think it through. If she had to, she'd nag him till he gave in, but she had a feeling she wouldn't have to.

All right, Dolly, he said at last. Gave her a sudden grin like a reckless boy's. I'll write to Arthur in the morning.

She thought, how little we know other people, no matter how closely we share our lives. There he is, that stick-in-the-mud who's never wanted to try anything new, but some hidden part of him has broken open, some adventurous part of him I never knew was there, and maybe he didn't either.

Their neighbours couldn't believe it. They were planted in the place, most of them without the education to do anything else. Happy to stay planted, happy to be stuck with whatever the weather threw at them. They might do a bit of whingeing about the drought or the floods, but couldn't see further than putting up with them.

Everyone chipped in and gave her and Bert a silver teapot as a going-away gift. They had it engraved: *Presented to Mr and Mrs Russell by their friends on leaving Gunnedah.* She was surprised, hadn't ever felt she and Bert had properly settled into being part of the Gunnedah world. She'd thought you had to be there thirty years, and care more about marmalade than she did, before that would happen. The teapot was probably more for Bert, she thought. He had that easy way with everyone, where she knew she could come across as a bit stiff.

◆

It was 1918 when they set off for Sydney, the war still going but swinging the right way at last. At Gunnedah Station the Russells' little pile of boxes and bags was pitiful after seven years without a crop. Arthur even had to wire them the money for the tickets.

Dolly hadn't seen him since they'd been at school together. When he met them at Central Station she wouldn't have recognised the grubby little boy in this big stout man, full-cheeked and prosperous-looking, his suit a bit too much of a good thing across the shoulders and a diamond tiepin flashing out of his shirt front.

Arthur had always been an outgoing talkative sort of person, not much like Bert in any way, and she wondered who Arthur's father was. The same as Bert's? She thought not, though you'd never know. But Arthur was like Bert in one way: his bluff cheery manner kept anything personal pushed well off to the side. He was a great one for the big hearty thing, pinching little Max's cheek. Sweet-natured Max, you could see he didn't like it, but he was a willing little lad, smiled at Arthur because he knew his noisy uncle was expecting a smile. Arthur ruffled Frank's mop of dark curls, made the same joke Dolly had heard so often: Oh Frank, looks like you're the black sheep of the family!

Oh, ho ho.

It was Nance's sixth birthday and Arthur gave her a shilling. You'd have thought the child had never seen money before, she was so thrilled, turned it over to inspect the ram on one side, the king's head on the other, and Dolly felt a spurt of anger. This difficult squinty frowning girl, smiling up at her uncle as if he was God come down to give her a pot of gold!

She got out her purse and fished out twenty-four half-pennies and whisked the shiny silver shilling away. Look, Nance, she said. I'll give you a lot more for your shilling!

Nance's little hands took the big brown coins reluctantly. You could see she had no interest in them, wanted the shilling back. But she said nothing. She had that way of closing down into herself.

Dolly was aware of Arthur watching her. Something about the set of his mouth told her he was seeing a side of his sister-in-law he didn't much like. There was nothing she could say—he'd got them the shop, they couldn't have done it without him. But who was he to judge her, she'd like to know. Just a bookie with his flash tiepin, making himself the big I-am with her daughter!

She wasn't going to let him know, but she saw she'd done the wrong thing. She hadn't liked Nance smiling at him in that radiant way, so she'd tried to best Arthur's gift with her own. Tried to make something more, when it was really less.

She nearly said, Oh, I'm sorry, Nance, of course you want the shiny one, pet! And given the shilling back to her. Could have put it right. But somehow the shilling was in her purse, the train was coming, everyone was moving, and in the fluster the moment was gone.

✦

The place Arthur had found for them was in a village called Wahroonga, at the northern end of the train line from Sydney. It was a sedate leafy area with rambling houses owned by rich people. But there was still plenty of bush around, and paddocks where people kept cows and grew vegetables. It was a soft landing, Dolly thought. Arthur was nobody's fool, he'd seen that the country mice should start in a way that wasn't too different from what they knew.

He'd gone through the books. The rent was reasonable, the takings steady. It looked like a good thing even for people with no experience of running a shop. He staked them for the bond and the first month's rent. After that, he made it clear, they'd be on their own.

The shop was a narrow place, the shop down below, two bedrooms up a steep flight of stairs, kitchen and the rest out the back. It was another world from the endless drudgery of the country. A gas stove, you just turned the knob and struck the match! Running water out of the tap! And a dunny out the back with a can under the seat, a man came every few days, took the full one away and left an empty one in its place. Threepence a week, she'd have happily paid ten times that. And no more having to milk the cow, because you bought your milk, fancy that. Bought your bacon and your soap and your bread. Let someone else do the hard work of making them.

The rich people had weekend places at Wahroonga, or substantial well-built houses with gables and verandahs, where the wife and children spent their days while the husband caught the train to work in the city. Behind hedges and tidy trees they led a second-hand English life, with swathes of lush lawns and rolled tennis courts.

Salubrious, that was the word Mrs Farquar used. She was one of their best customers, so you nodded when Mrs Farquar held forth in her loud way, even if *salubrious* wasn't a word you'd ever heard before. The air so much more salubrious, Mrs Russell, and the children thriving so well.

Women like Mrs Farquar could have sent the kitchen maid down to the shop for butter and sugar, but the wives were bored at home all day behind their lawns and empty tennis courts. Going down to the Russells' shop made an outing.

Dolly thought she could have charged them anything. It all went on tick—they called it *the account*—and at the end of the month the husband would come and pay it off.

They spoke nicely and you could tell they'd never done a hand's turn, like that Miss Mackellar up at Kurrumbede. Another species almost, with their lovely clothes, and so careless with them, their hems drooping in the dirt and mud all over their lovely kid shoes. They'd leave their gloves behind, and when Dolly kept them under the counter and gave them back the next time, they took them with only a casual thank-you, but Dolly had seen those gloves at Mark Foy's, knew they cost three guineas.

And why could they be so casual? Only because their fathers were rich. A rich father, and then they got a rich husband who was looking for a wife with the right manner, someone who'd grown up learning how to manage a big house and servants and how to entertain in style. A wife who, if she had difficult children, wasn't driven to thinking about drowning them in the horse trough, because there'd be a nursemaid to look after them. The children in turn would go to the expensive schools where they'd meet people from the same world. That whole set of people marrying each other and keeping it going, generation after generation.

When she, Dolly Russell, was as good as them! Had more brains than most of them, she knew, but had the luck of the draw to be born a Maunder in little Currabubula, where the publican was the top of the pecking order. By golly, if she had a silk dress like theirs, and those lovely kid shoes, she'd show them the respect of looking after them. And she wouldn't sit on her backside all day doing cross-stitch and complaining about the servants.

They were all rich, but there were one or two who weren't silvertails. There was Mrs Turner, a plain stout woman with frizzy red hair. The Turners had plenty of money, but you could tell from the way Mrs Turner spoke, and the way she looked pretty sharply at everything before she bought it, that she wasn't from old money. She liked to pass the time leaning up at the counter with Dolly, and Dolly always enjoyed a gasbag with her because they came from the same world. Mrs Turner had grown up at Werris Creek, just down the road from Curra, her dad a fettler.

Her husband had made his pile in tallow. There's money in muck, Mrs Turner liked to say. Money in muck, and better to have it than not, wouldn't you agree, Mrs Russell?

Dolly guessed she was probably sick of the other ladies' squeezed little smiles and the way they were suddenly in a rush when they came into the shop and found Mrs Turner there. They'd think she was vulgar, what they'd call *ill bred*. Yes, Dolly supposed Mrs Turner was vulgar, but the diamonds in her brooch were real.

And she was a happy woman. They had a brood of cheerful healthy children and made the most of their money. Their middle boy, a bright spark, was off to Newington College in the city. The best education money can buy! Mrs Turner said. We'll send him as a boarder so he can pick up, you know, a bit of polish. He won't never get it from me and Ern! Laughed her stout woman's loud jolly laugh, she didn't care.

The other side of Bert's secretive way was this surprise: he had a nice manner behind a counter, knew how to butter up all those rich women. For someone who knew him as well as Dolly did, that hail-fellow-well-met manner was just another way for him to hide who he was, but he'd get the women laughing, she'd see him twinkling his blue eyes at them and they'd twinkle right back and go off smiling. They'd be at the counter again soon, though, they'd forgotten they needed half a pound of raisins. Oh Mr Russell, I'd forget my head if it wasn't screwed on! You'd think that was the funniest thing Bert had ever heard.

Dolly served in the shop when Bert was doing the deliveries, enjoyed the give and take, the rich women rippling along in their silk and the maids who knew their mistress's little secrets. She loved the feeling of life surging through the shop, so different from those long silent days on the farm with only a sheep bleating and the crows scrabbling on the roof.

The train station was just across the road from the shop and once a week she'd go into the city. Getting out, a change of scene: that was a luxury she'd never had. Oh, she loved the bustle and rush of town, the feeling of life being lived at a faster pace, the windows full of things you'd never buy but loved to look at, above all the sense that no one knew who you were. What freedom there was in that, after spending your life among people who knew you, knew where you came from, knew what you wanted and what you couldn't have. On the streets of Sydney she was just another small woman in a squashed-looking brown hat. No one knew anything about her and no one cared. It was as good as being invisible.

She could even go away at the weekends and in the school holidays, just her and the children. They tried the Blue Mountains a few times, the famous Three Sisters at Katoomba and the rest of it, but it was all depressing mist and too many waterfalls. But once they'd tried the beach they kept going back: Mrs Woodford's Beach House at Newport, out on a long peninsula with the ocean on one side and the calm stretch of Pittwater on the other. Sometimes Bert came, but more often he stayed behind. Someone had to mind the shop.

They were in the dining room at Beach House when Mrs Woodford rushed in with a telegram in her hand. It's over, she cried out, her voice all trembly and strange. It's over, they've signed the armistice!

That night everyone went down to the beach, there was a gigantic bonfire on the sand, the children were goggle-eyed at it all, Nance and Frank running backwards and forwards throwing more wood on the bonfire, and some woman who evidently had a son or a husband away fighting, on her knees in the sand with her hands up shouting, Thank you God, thank you God! while all around people were letting off crackers and blurting great blasts of noise on cornets and drums. A new start, it felt like, for the whole world.

✦

Frank and Nance were old enough for school now, went off

every morning to the public school at Warrawee. It wasn't where the children of the rich folk went, of course, they went to private schools. But Warrawee Public did the job, the same way Currabubula Public had. Frank came home with his reader, still the same one she and Bert had used, fancy that, and Nance was soon spelling out the words on the biscuit tin.

Having them at school, with just easygoing little Max at home, made life so much simpler. Something had never come right between her and the oldest two. She couldn't find a way to be an easy mother with them and she knew they were a bit frightened of her, frightened of the flame of anger in her that they'd seen a few times too often. They were close to each other, but not to her. She'd hear them whispering and giggling together, and she'd say, Come on, let me in on the joke! She'd be trying to set things on a different track, where she could sidestep the anger and get to the love. The love was there, but somehow it was hard to bring it out. But they'd close down against her, obstinate, pushing her away, and she'd be hurt, and angry all over again.

Women were supposed to love being mothers, it was supposed to come naturally to them and give them all they wanted, but she knew in her private heart that it wasn't that way for her. Perhaps some women just weren't cut out to be mothers. Or perhaps it was what had happened at the start, when her own misery and confusion and rage had stained the way she felt about those children born into the middle of her unhappiness, the way a bit of beetroot stained an apron.

One night she saw Frank and Nance watching as Bert

hoisted Max up onto his shoulders, the little boy so thrilled to be up near the ceiling, going up the stairs to bed. Come along, possum, Bert said, his big hands holding the chubby feet beside his chin, the tenderness naked in his voice.

Frank looked away but Nance kept on staring. Dolly could see her wondering in her child's way, Why not me too? Not their fault, but they were out in the cold, and already it seemed too late to put it right.

✦

There was just one drawback to the shop: being with Bert all the time. At Rothesay she'd had time to herself, Bert out in the paddocks or away for weeks at a time shearing. When he was away it was as good as being a widow. Now he was never away, he was every day in the shop and every night in the bed that sagged in the middle so no matter how you tried you couldn't stop rolling into each other.

As for what went on with her and Bert in the bed—well, it was never the radiant thing it had been with Jim. She thought you probably only got that once in your life, that mysterious coming-together of who knows what, something that took two bodies and made them into one ecstatic mindless panting creature. For a teasing moment she could sometimes get a flicker of that with Bert. She didn't mind it if she was in the mood. But Bert was always in the mood.

There were women who went on having children until their change of life but she wasn't going to be one of them.

97

Three was enough. She'd been under the thumb of her parents all those years, and now she was under another kind of thumb, looking after the children. She hadn't had a turn at living yet, and she was already thirty-six.

Now that she was in Sydney she'd found out about a few things you couldn't get in Gunnedah. Little sponges on strings that you soaked in vinegar. Some big pill things called The Housewife's Friend. You didn't swallow them, you put them up yourself. They were better than nothing, but they couldn't be trusted. Every night was a lottery. Every night when Bert reached for her, she thought, Will another one start tonight? At Newport she remembered how good it was to have the bed to herself. That was another kind of holiday.

She knew she'd done the right thing getting them away from that bloody farm. She did the books, Bert left all that to her, and they were making money hand over fist. She couldn't believe how it added up, a penny here, a halfpenny there.

It was so different from the farm, where you could decide when to sow the wheat, and which paddock to sow it in, but after that it was out of your hands. It might rain at the right time, or it might not. Wheat prices might hold, or they might fall. There was nothing you could do about any of it. Whereas in a shop you could keep track of which lines sold best and order more. Work out which things you could put the biggest markup on. Arrange a pyramid of boxes nicely, or a fan of packets, and put them where the customers could see them so they'd think, Ooh, I'll have one of those too.

You could make a mistake, order too much of something

and have to throw it out, but it was your mistake, and you learned from it. You made sure you did better the next time. Whether you did well or badly, it was up to you.

Still, they were coming to the end of ways they could build up the business. Wahroonga was a backwater. Their customers were good, but there'd never be many more of them. And now that the shop was going as well as it could, there were days when the deadly familiarity of everything drove her dilly. She thought, This could be my life for the rest of my days, old Mr and Mrs Russell in the grocery store. There she was, a woman in her prime, playing second fiddle to her husband in a little dead-and-alive shop, when she knew she could do so much more.

You could sit on what you had, or you could turn what you had into something bigger. You just had to be prepared to take a bit of a risk.

✦

When Mrs Woodford complained one day that she was too old to be running a boarding-house and was looking for someone to take over the lease, Dolly knew straightaway she'd do it. There weren't many businesses a woman could do on her own, but running a boarding-house was one. She could see already how easy it would be to turn Beach House into a goldmine. Some fresh paint, get a good cook, and dart about, the way Mrs Woodford was too old to do, making sure all the weekend visitors felt a bit cossetted. Bert could stay on at the shop and join them at the weekends. Two businesses, twice the money, and she'd be out of that little shop, that little stuffy bedroom.

She thought about how to put it to Bert, how to flatter or coax. *Over my dead body.* That kind of answer was always on the cards because, when push came to shove, it would be his name—the man's name—on the lease.

In the end she came straight out with it, blunt and unsoftened. Mrs Woodford's selling up at Beach House, she said. Why don't I take it over? You stay here during the week, come down to Newport for the weekends.

She had to give this to Bert: he wasn't a man to go against something just because it was a woman suggesting it. He saw immediately how it would work, didn't take much persuading. Frank and Nance were the problem. They grizzled and grizzled about the move. We like it here, Mum, Frank said, and Nance put on her sulking face.

Don't be ridiculous, Dolly said, you love it at the beach!

They were frightened of change, she supposed that was the way children were. But they'd soon settle at the new school and make new friends. They were only children, didn't know how things worked. You couldn't let them run your life.

Dolly found a good woman to do the meals, Mrs Cook, funny wasn't it. Mrs Cook ran a good kitchen as long as Dolly kept her well stocked with fresh food and slipped her a bottle of sherry for herself once a week. There was a housemaid, and when things were busy a couple of local girls came along, cash in hand, to help out. Beach House was full every weekend.

Bert closed the shop early on a Friday afternoon, got the

train to Milson's Point, the tram to Narrabeen and then the bus up to Newport. It took him a good while, but he didn't mind. He'd be at Newport for Friday and Saturday nights, buttering up all the guests, then go back to Wahroonga on Sunday night, ready to open the shop on Monday morning.

The children loved having Bert at the weekends. He was a good father, had the knack with children. She thought he must have learned that from Henry Newitt. He must have been a good stepfather. Bert took the children swimming, built them a treehouse, played cricket with them. No wonder he was their favourite! He wasn't the one who had to nag them to brush their teeth and pick up after themselves.

Frank and Nance were at Newport Public School, just the one room like at Curra, the kids all crammed in along the benches so they hardly had room to lift their elbows to write, and not enough of anything so they had to take turns with the readers. But they were happy enough, running barefoot up the sandy path to school every morning. The good thing about the crowded room was that when Mr Barnes asked Nance how to spell *indeed*, Frank was close enough to whisper the answer to her, and that made everyone happy.

❖

Since the business of the locked trunk, Dolly had only seen her parents when she couldn't get out of it. A few family Christmases, Sonny's wedding. Once the Russells had left Gunnedah and went to the city it was easier to make an excuse.

Dolly had been at Beach House a few months when Eddie wrote to say their mother was very sick and, Dolly, I think you'd best see her. Then a day later another note, their mother had gone down to a hospital in Manly that someone had told her about.

Manly wasn't far from Newport. Each day Dolly thought, I'll go tomorrow. But the idea of her mother sick, or in hospital—and just down the road in Manly!—was hard to believe. It was too different from the picture of the strong stern woman that lived in a dark unhappy locked-away part of Dolly's memory.

So it was bewildering to arrive at the hospital at last and see this shrunken person curled up on the bed with a white face and vague eyes. Dolly had to check the board above the bed, *Sarah Catherine Maunder*, because this wasn't her mother. She had no fight with this poor scrap of old woman.

She sat by the bed, held the thin dry hand for a while, steadied the glass to help her drink. Stayed a long time in a kind of blankness while Sarah Catherine Maunder breathed and sighed and now and then plucked at the sheet. Late in the day Dolly went out into the sunshine, into the rude vigour of the wind and the surf. She wouldn't visit again. Behind her in the hospital bed was a soul making her way out of the world, but the person on that journey was a stranger to Dolly.

Everyone came down to Manly for the funeral, the brothers and their wives, the sisters and their husbands. She had to look twice to recognise her father. It was the dark suit, but it was something else too, something uncertain, something tentative, like a man who could see all right but couldn't make sense of what he was seeing. When he glanced around at Dolly he didn't quite catch her eye, she had to go right up to him and touch him on the arm, and she was glad Eddie and Sonny were there doing all the talking that had to be done.

The women—her sisters and sisters-in-law—were glancing about, excited in spite of the solemn occasion. They didn't often get away from the country and it was a sparkling day, the sea glittering and the gulls soaring. For those people the city was a glamorous foreign country, but for Dolly it was home. It was good to see her brothers, good to see Rose and Sophia, but they were people from far away and long ago.

As they started on the last hymn something suddenly climbed up, some great choking obstruction, into Dolly's throat. She heard herself make a wordless cry that was like a child protesting. Her eyes ached with sudden tears, and harsh blurting gulps and cries forced their way out of some great fist that was twisting her in its grip.

Later she thought, Was that grief? Was it sadness? Sadness was soft, surely. Grief was soft. What had taken her over had no softness to it, no sweetly melancholy mourning. It was harder than that. This was a rough pain, and it wasn't about having lost her mother. It was about never having known her, and never having been known by her. That was the loss: the loss of something never found.

Her father must have been grieving, she thought, though with a rock like him you'd never know. Had they loved each other, her mother and father? Taken pleasure in coming together to make their children? Or had it been, as it looked from the outside, a relationship of severity, self-control, joyless-ness?

He'd stay on Forest Farm, she supposed, till he got too old to manage. Rose would be the one who'd have to deal with him. Dolly didn't envy her that job, saving the pride of that hard old man.

◆

As Mrs Russell of Beach House, she found a sociable outgoing person in herself. When things weren't too busy she'd sit down for a game of euchre with the regulars. Have a drink and a cigarette once tea was over and she could hear the washing-up being done out in the kitchen.

She loved Newport, loved the smell of the sea and the rush and whisper of the surf all night through the open window. Its restlessness met some restlessness in herself that was soothed by it.

Still, once everything was running along smoothly she started to get sick of the boarding-house, the same way she'd got sick of the grocery, and the farm before that. Once you'd fixed everything up and got a place as good as you could, there was no interest in it. Six or eight months down the track at Beach House, all you had to deal with was guests grizzling about there not being enough hot water, or turning up their noses at Mrs Cook's jam roly-poly, and where was the pleasure in that?

Then one of the weekend guests made a throwaway remark.

Oh, your husband, Mrs Russell, this woman exclaimed. She was flushed, Dolly saw, a bit flustered. What a handsome man he is, oh you must miss him when he goes back to Wahroonga! It's a long week, isn't it, all on your own?

Dolly could see the woman wasn't trying to tell her anything, probably didn't even realise what her flush and fluster was giving away. She'd caught Bert's twinkling eye and she'd twinkled back, that was all. No harm in that, and if Bert's charm brought in customers to the boarding-house the way he brought them to the grocery, that was all right.

Still, the woman had crystallised what Dolly had been hardly aware of knowing. Now she looked at it square-on: there was her husband, that handsome man. He'd twinkled away at her, back when he was courting. Done a lot more than twinkle at that Beth. And at the shop there were all those women, the ladies and their maids. He'd be twinkling away at them all week. He'd close the shop at five o'clock and what happened then? A long night ahead of him, all on his own?

She was in a bit of a corner. She could get away from Bert by being somewhere else. It was what she'd done when she'd stayed and stayed at Dorrigo. But she had to remember what had happened then. If she was away too much, she might find herself in a worse kind of trouble.

With a pulse of excitement, she thought: We'll sell up. Sell the grocery and sell the boarding-house, use the money to get a bigger business. But not another grocery, not another boarding-house.

1919

The Goodwill

WHEN she showed Bert the newspaper advertisement, the Crown Hotel in Camden, he wasn't sure.

Oh, I don't know, Dolly, he said. Aren't we well enough as we are? Do we want to stick our necks out?

Yes, and never get on, she said, in a rage of impatience with his farmer's caution. Sit like bloody tadpoles in a puddle!

But she could see he was going to be hard to budge, so she went into town to have a word with his brother Arthur. As a bookie he knew you had to risk money to make it, and Bert would be swayed by him. She and Arthur had tea at Cahill's. He listened, looked at the numbers she'd come up with.

So you reckon Bert's got to be talked around, eh, he said.

And you reckon I'll be the one to do it.

She smiled. In another life she and Arthur could have made a good team.

My word, Dolly, he said, half-admiring but half-rueful too. My word, you're a canny one, no two ways about that.

※

Camden was a village on the southern outskirts of Sydney, and the Crown was a humble little pub on the last street, where the houses tailed off into paddocks. It was dairying country and the Crown was where the cow-cockies dropped in to have a beer after work, the mud still on their boots.

But Dolly could see what the previous owners couldn't, how to build it up. It was 1919, the war and the Spanish Flu were over, and people were starting to tour about in their cars and charabancs. The Burragorang Valley down the road was a favourite sightseeing place. You'd do lunches for the tourists, put a sign out the front, something like *Gateway to the Valley*.

The children were cranky when she told them they'd be moving again. They'd liked Mrs Cook, she was forever spoiling them with treats in the kitchen, and they'd loved the water and the beach. Well, they couldn't see beyond the pleasure of the moment. It was up to the adults to make the decisions.

Frank and Nance went to the one-room school in Camden village. Max wanted to go too, but he was only four. He'd wait all day by the gate for them to come home and when they did, he wouldn't let up pestering them. Why couldn't he have a turn on the billycart? Why couldn't he go down the creek with them? They'd go off together and he'd run along after. *Wait for me! Wait for me!* If Dolly made them take him along she'd end up wishing she hadn't, because there'd always be something he came running home crying about: a cut knee, a spider bite, a broken tooth. So she got a girl from the village to come afternoons and evenings, when Dolly and Bert were flat out, to give the children their dinner and keep the peace.

At her mother's funeral, her brother Eddie had urged her to send Nance to a convent school. For a girl, he said, the nuns gave the best education. He was sending his daughters to board with the nuns at the Gunnedah Convent school and they were coming on a treat, he said. They didn't take any notice of all the Catholic nonsense.

She'd met Dulcie and Phyllis at the funeral, and it was true, they were mature for their years, nicely turned out, knew how to make a bit of conversation with their aunt. She'd thought of Nance, not that much younger than they were, running a bit wild at Camden Public, another overcrowded government school where the teacher had his hands too full to make sure everyone was coming along as well as they should. Well, Nance was only seven. Camden Public would do for the time being, but she tucked the idea away in the back of her mind, what Eddie had said about the nuns.

✦

As Bert had charmed the ladies and their maids at Wahroonga, he charmed the tourists at Camden. In the Ladies' Lounge he put on a bit of a show, setting the drinks down with a dangerous-looking flourish. Where had he learned those fancy ways with a tray of drinks, Dolly wondered. Is that what his father was like: a smiling man who could carry a tray full of drinks as if it was no heavier than a newspaper, swooping it down, the glasses staying put through the speed of the movement, and then set them down on the table with not a drop spilled, so the ladies went ooh and aah?

She saw him twinkling away at them and the brassy ones gave him a look straight back into the twinkle. There was a twist of something bitter in her heart when she saw how the ladies loved him. But they'd be on their way soon, and she knew they'd spread the word. Oh, if you're going through Camden, don't miss the Crown!

He was good with the men in the bar, too. The customer was always right, of course. Until he wasn't. When there was a bad drunk starting to make trouble, Bert showed the other side of himself. The boy who'd beaten up Ted Abbott had grown into this man, very calm, not saying much, getting the drunk's arm up behind his back and marching him out the door, having a word with him in the yard. Next day, more often than not, the man would come up to Dolly. Make my apologies, Mrs Russell, he'd mumble. One too many. Won't happen again.

One good thing about a pub was that it had plenty of bedrooms. She and Bert each had their own. Bert came in when he needed to, got in the bed with her. It was what rich people did, she'd learned that at Wahroonga. Those women all had their own bedroom and the husband had to come through something called a dressing room to get to it.

She didn't serve behind the bar unless things were very busy. Bert said he didn't want her to do that. The Crown wasn't the best pub in the village but it was a matter of raising the standard, and part of that was having the publican's wife dignified behind the till rather than slopping out beer.

He didn't exactly dress up to serve behind the bar but he always had a waistcoat and jacket on, and the watch chain with the watch that he checked for closing time, and his boots were always well shined even though the customers didn't see them. He'd always had a touch of the dandy. When he was working for her father she'd thought that was silly, but it was paying off now. The Crown was starting to look like a place with a bit of class.

The tourists were good business, but only when the weather was good. In the heat of summer and the mud of winter they wouldn't come. Dolly saw they'd have to get something more dependable. That meant getting the reps, the travelling salesmen. They usually stayed at the Royal in the middle of the town, it suited them because it was close to the shops, so you'd have to put a bit of work in to lure them away. She took out some space in the *Camden News*, made sure the bit about *Special Rate for Representatives* was in big letters. Bert wasn't sure about giving the reps such a big discount, but she knew the extra business would soon pay for itself. It would make the place look wide awake, and a bustling pub would attract more business.

The Royal had a room where the reps laid out their samples—well, the Crown could go one better. She talked Bert into doing up the shed at the back, putting in some big tables where the things could be displayed to best advantage. And she was always on the spot at breakfast time. She served the reps herself, made a bit of a fuss of them. Put an extra rasher on their plate and make sure they noticed.

Bert was always behind the bar but Dolly was everywhere, helping Mrs Harrington with the beds and the laundry when they'd had a lot of weekend guests, popping in and out of the kitchen. She was run off her feet but she loved being on the go all day. At last she had her hand on the levers that directed her life. She'd got them off that damned hopeless farm. She'd got them out of the dead-and-alive shop. She'd turned Beach House into good money. She could see how to get on, and she was pretty sure now that she could always wear Bert down to get what she wanted. For the first time in her life she could have a dream and—through nothing but her own brains and will—make it happen.

As the place got busier, Bert thought they should get more help. Another maid to work with Mrs Harrington, a girl to help behind the bar. She hardly let him finish before she said no, they didn't need anyone, and he rolled his eyes.

Oh, come on Dolly, he said, we've got the money, you don't have to make a bloody martyr of yourself!

I'm the one thinking about this family, she shot back, her voice rising. This is our chance to make some money for once in our bloody lives, Bert Russell, and by God I'm not going to throw it away on some girl when I can do it myself in half the time!

That was true. But she listened to herself filling the air with words, and knew there was a picture behind them that she wasn't going to look at straight: *some girl*, and Bert watching her.

❖

Next door to the Crown there was a hall with a rollerskating rink. Frank and Nance were heading off there one day with their sixpences when Nance suddenly turned back to Dolly and said, Come on Mum! Come with us! I dare you!

Cheeky, but apprehensive too. Dolly knew in a flare of understanding that it was just how she'd watched her own mother and father, that mix of love and fear. It was the boldness in Nance's little face, the boldness and apprehension both at once, that made Dolly want to go out to meet her, one person offering a hand to another.

She wasn't going to strap on skates but she went in with them and leaned on the rail to watch. She could feel how the speed of the passing skaters made a breeze in her hair, and was frightened, but thrilled too, at the speed and the noise, the rumble of so many wheels flicking and grinding against the dirt on the wooden floor and girls screaming in the racket. There they were, coming round, Frank and Nance hand in hand. She smiled at them through the crowd and saw Nance's face light up with a sudden surprised smile back.

She waited. There was some kind of chance being offered, some breaking of the habit between her and her daughter, and after a time Nance skated over.

Frank's with Clive and the others, she said, and didn't need to say, *They don't want a girl with them.*

She took off her skates and they went out into the cool under the trees. The afternoon sun was slanting across so there was a long wobbly line of fence drawn in shadow on the grass, and for once a companiable feeling between mother and daughter.

Want a pear, Mum? Nance asked.

She didn't wait for Dolly to answer, was shimmying up the old tree like a monkey, Dolly could see her brown legs all the way up to her bloomers. Opened her mouth to say, Get down this minute, Nance, there you are showing the world your bloomers! But shut it again. That was what you were supposed to say, to stop a girl doing anything lively. But if Nance wanted to climb the tree and get her mother a pear, well, what was wrong with a girl's legs?

They stood there together with the pear juice running down their chins, a big smudge on Nance's face where pear juice and dirt had stuck.

I'll always remember this, Mum, Nance said, and Dolly knew that she was storing away the rare moment of ease between them. But why so rare? Why so little ease?

She's got plenty of go in her, Dolly thought, and for once she felt tender towards this difficult girl. Still, there was a rueful edge to the tenderness. Here the child was, happy in her skin, no idea of what was ahead of her, the battles ahead of any girl. Could she protect her? Give her the armour she'd need? Nothing in her own life showed her what a mother might do for a daughter. She'd have to make it up as she went along.

◆

Rose wrote, a laboured note. Poor thing, she could barely put a sentence together. Her eldest, Edna, was keen on one of the Scott boys, she said. Presbyterian, of course. They were walking out together secretly, they thought no one knew. Could Dolly see her way clear to taking Edna on as a barmaid for a while? A bit of distance might make the thing fade away.

It wouldn't be Rose who was worried about a Presbyterian for her daughter, Dolly thought. It might be Catholic Ted, even though he hadn't minded getting a C of E girl up the duff. Or maybe it was the Scotts, they were very staunch Presbyterians and they mightn't want their boy mixed up with a Catholic. Oh, bloody religion, Dolly thought. All those lives mucked up.

Edna was a bright hardworking girl, eighteen and well able to look after herself behind the bar, not that the men gave her any lip with Bert working alongside her. She knew her own mind, a clear-headed young woman. She and the Scott boy were just biding their time, Dolly could see, till they were of age. Good on them both for being braver than Jim Murphy.

◆

Dolly was starting to understand that living in a pub wasn't like living in a boarding-house. At Beach House the guests had been mostly families or young couples. But at the Crown it was mostly men, and they were there to drink. If they got too rowdy Bert got rid of them, but there'd be shouting and singing and there'd be a fair bit of ripe language. Every night there'd be some fellow who couldn't find the dunny in the dark and pissed in the yard instead. The children would come home from school and there'd be some bloke giving them pennies to make them dance. She put a stop to any of that nonsense quick smart, of course. But they were living in a place where there was always a drunk around, and she couldn't be everywhere at once.

Then one day Nance came to her, told her Jemmy Finney had found her in the laundry, got between her and the door and pulled his thing out of his pants and flapped it at her. Nance wasn't upset exactly, but she'd got a fright, knew there was something nasty about it. Wanted to know what the thing was and why had Jemmy waggled it at her?

No harm done. Jemmy Finney was a poor silly fellow, a brick short of a full load. He wouldn't have done anything, not really. But it was a warning. You couldn't have a girl growing up in that atmosphere.

When she told Bert about Jemmy he jumped up so fast the chair fell over backwards with a clatter. If Jemmy had been there, Dolly thought, Bert would have ripped his thing right off. But it wasn't about Jemmy. It was the whole situation: drunks and children too close to each other.

Bert's answer was to go back to a shop, or find another boarding-house. But Dolly couldn't bear the thought. There was no scope with a shop or boarding-house. Whereas here she'd been thinking about knocking a doorway through from the bar, building an extension out the side, she'd call it the Snug, like in an English pub. Leather armchairs, pictures of sailing ships. Toby jugs. She couldn't go backwards! They'd only just got going!

When Edna goes home we'll send Nance with her, she said. To Curra. She can stay with Rose and Ted, go to school there for a while.

Oh, what's the point of that, Dolly, Bert said. We can't leave her there forever, what do we do when she comes back?

He had that wooden look, the look he got on the rare times he set himself against her.

Oh, I don't know, Bert, she shouted. I don't bloody know, so don't bloody ask me!

He registered that she wasn't going to back down. They knew each other so well now. It took hardly the barest movement of a muscle around the mouth to know what the other was thinking.

Look, Bert, I don't know, she said. But she can't stay here with fellers flashing their willies at her. We'll work something out. But I am not going back to some bloody shop, I can tell you that now.

Of course Nance made a fuss, didn't want to go.

It'll be an adventure, Nance, Dolly told her. You'll love it!

But seeing Nance's frightened white face at the train

window, she nearly changed her mind. The image stayed with Dolly for the rest of the day, a stain through every hour.

Rose sent word, Nance was loving it at Curra, she'd been picked to be Little Red Riding Hood in the school play, and she was a darling to have about the place.

A darling! Oh, Rose had always been a soft touch.

✦

They'd been at the Crown just on a year when one of the reps happened to mention that the licence for the Federal Hotel in Campbelltown was for sale. Even as the man was still talking, Dolly made up her mind to go and look at it, and she came home knowing they ought to take it. Campbelltown was closer to Sydney, more go-ahead than Camden, and on the train line. The Federal was on the best street, a stone's throw from the station. Much better than the Crown: eighteen rooms, plus a long room for banquets and dances. Best of all, the private quarters were well away from the public area, so there'd be no need for the children to go anywhere near the bar. This time Bert didn't object. She thought he fancied himself in charge of a bustling important place.

During the sale of the shop, Dolly had learned that when you put a business on the market you weren't just selling the lease. You were also selling something she'd never heard of before: the *goodwill*. The goodwill wasn't something you could hold in your hand. It was an invisible thing, a service. You built a business up by persuading more customers to buy from you.

118

When you sold, the *goodwill* those customers felt towards your business was one of the things you were selling.

Building the goodwill had cost you nothing. The only outlay was your own energy and charm. But later on you could put a value on the goodwill, actual pounds and shillings. It was like the compound interest that Mr Murray had explained: something for nothing, a kind of magic.

They'd built up the Crown the same way they'd built up the shop, and Dolly knew they'd make a good profit when they sold. Knowing that gave her a deep pleasure, a satisfaction and a feeling of completeness that she'd never felt before. The good feeling wasn't about the things she'd be able to buy, though fine kid shoes were nice to have. It wasn't about having the money and spending it. It was about making it. She was learning this about herself: she loved planning a thing, thinking her way around all the corners, making it work. It was as if there was a muscle in your head for thinking, and it liked to be used, the way the muscles in your legs liked to go for a walk.

✦

The first big do they had in the long room at the Federal was a banquet for the Campbelltown centenary celebrations. Dolly made sure the man from the *News* had a seat at the top table and sent over a bottle of the best for him and the photographer, so there was a good splash in the paper next day about the go-ahead new management of *one of Campbelltown's premier establishments.*

The centenary was a lot of hoo-ha about nothing, Dolly thought, but it was good for business. The Federal was right on the route of the parade and the balconies were crowded with people watching the floats and cheering, so the pub was in the background of all the newspaper photos, the sign standing out nice and clear. Dolly went to the newspaper office, got enlarged prints made and hung them up in the bar. It was surprising how many people came in specially to see them, and once people were standing in a bar of course they'd have a few drinks.

She had to accept that she and Bert needed plenty of staff to run such a large place, but she made sure she was the one who interviewed the girls. Some of them came all gussied up for the interview. More fool you, she thought. She went for the plain ones, and even plain as they were she kept them under her thumb. There was pretty quick turnover of housemaids at the Federal. Oh Mrs Russell, she can't keep good staff, she imagined people saying, and she answered them in her mind. Well, perhaps I don't want to.

She wouldn't have barmaids, but Bert had a couple of barmen. They were lively young fellows, didn't mind teasing Mrs Russell, but she could see them treading carefully. Bert's a good bloke, she could imagine them telling each other. But best go a bit steady with that missus of his.

She didn't care. She was paying them. They didn't have to like her.

✦

They left Nance at Curra with Rose for the better part of a year. When she joined them at the Federal it was *Auntie Rose this* and *Auntie Rose that*, so much that Dolly felt a pang—it was almost as if the girl thought Rose was her mother!

Nance was nearly nine. She'd come back home unsettled: cheeky or tearful or retreating into the sulks. The sulks made the rage rise up in Dolly like water filling a glass, rage that had nowhere to go, because there was nothing you could do if a child met you with the turning-away, the cast-down eyes, the obstinate chin.

And wilful. Nance would make up her mind about some silly thing and not rest till she got it. They sent her to the local school with Frank and Max and she made friends with a girl who came to school barefoot. Nance got it into her head that she wanted to do the same. Nothing Dolly could do, not coaxing, not shouting, not slapping, not locking her in her room, would make her put her shoes on. The child was strong, couldn't be forced, and by God she was stubborn. As stubborn—Dolly had to admit—as she was herself.

But she would not let her daughter go to school barefoot. She would not. That was a slide backwards. She would not let that be done to her.

You deal with her, Bert, she said. I've had enough.

She thought he might take Nance's side. After all, he'd sat in the classroom at Curra all those years with his dirty feet bare on the boards. She was ready for him to say, What's the harm in bare feet? Was ready for a fight. Half wanted it. But he wasn't going to give her one.

All right, Dolly, he said, mild as water, and went away to Nance's room. She never knew what he said, but from then on the girl wore her shoes to school. Dolly was left with her feelings boiling up inside with nowhere to go. It was a win, but somehow it didn't feel like one.

◆

When they'd sold the lease of the Crown, Dolly realised that being in business wasn't like being on a farm, where you stayed your whole life. For the magic of the goodwill to work, you had to keep moving, had to keep buying and selling. If you stayed in one place you'd have the day-to-day income from your business, but you'd never get that lump sum, that capital. You never just sat on the capital. You kept using it, like a lever, to get more. She had a picture of herself with her hand warm and confident on a great metal handle.

And moving suited her. She loved to feel that she could get up and go any time she liked. The stifled feeling that you were stuck in one place was a kind of horror that went back, she supposed, to those long failed years at Rothesay, and before that to the dusty paddocks of Forest Farm, that there'd seemed no way of getting away from.

Women were supposed to be homebodies, happy with their little round of hearth and family, and plenty of them were. Good luck to them. But Dolly knew she was made differently. She wanted something—what it was, she couldn't say exactly—something bigger, more surprising, maybe even more dangerous.

So, although things were going full steam ahead at the Federal, by late in 1921 she was glancing through the back pages of the newspaper again. There it was one day: *Licence and Lease for Sale, The Queensland Hotel, Temora.*

Temora was a sizeable town three hundred miles south-west of Sydney. In the past it had grown rich on gold, and when the gold ran out it stayed rich on great crops of wheat. There was plenty of money in Temora, and the Queensland by all accounts was one of the best hotels in the town.

The craving for a new place, a new venture, a new set of challenges to meet and conquer—once that craving gripped her she couldn't ignore it. And now her restlessness, seemingly as fixed in her as the colour of her eyes, could be justified by the truth about how business worked. That friendly word *goodwill*, and behind it the powerful idea of *capital*.

She and Bert went through the numbers, heads together at the bar after closing time, a glass of whisky at his elbow and a Pimm's at hers. These were their best times together, Dolly thought. It mightn't be Romeo and Juliet but they were a good business partnership.

Next day he took the train to see the place, sent a telegram to say he'd put the deposit down. When he came back he couldn't stop talking about it. A top place, Temora, he said, and the Queensland was right in the middle of town, wrapped around the corner of the two main streets. Iron lace and a wide verandah. Enormous high-ceilinged rooms with fanlights over the doors. Silk bedspreads in every room. Like the Cally, he said. Nearly as good as that.

The children listened, and finally Frank said, It's good here, Mum. Why do we have to up sticks again?

She had a moment's fluster. Were they doing the right thing after all?

Don't be cheeky, Frank, she said, and saw him shrink into himself, felt a bully's nasty satisfaction. That's what we're doing and there's nothing more to be said.

But Nance was pushing her chair back from the table with a huge scraping noise. They all sat listening to her run up the stairs and slam the door to her room so hard that a few flecks of paint floated down from the ceiling.

Dolly tried to find a different tone. Look, Frank, she said, it'll be so much better, you'll see—the opportunities! You'll thank me for it later.

But he wouldn't look at her, and she felt her anger rise. He never argued, the way Nance did, but never agreed either. He'd become a watchful boy. He'd say nothing, then turn away. Who was he, just a child, to sit there in that sulky way, making her feel in the wrong? And his sister, storming off, trying to make them change their minds?

1922

How To Be a Spinster

TEMORA was a flat spread-out place with the wide streets that the old-time bullockies had needed for carting the wool and wheat. Some lovely buildings, thanks to the gold-rush money: a bank with stone columns and curlicues like a Greek temple, the post office elegant with contrasting brickwork and fancy curves.

There at the centre of it, at the heart of the town, was the Queensland Hotel. It was just as Bert had promised, nearly as good as the Cally. The same wide verandah edged with iron lace, thick barley-twist metal columns, generous windows and doors. A fanlight over every door to keep things cool in summer and a fireplace in every room for the cold winters. Nothing skimped, nothing improvised, no shabby corners. You could go anywhere, even out in the yard, lift anything up and look under it and it was all of a piece: clean, orderly, best quality. It had a good class of clientele. You didn't go to the Queensland in your muddy boots.

Temora was prime wheat country. As there'd been at Gunnedah, there were people in Temora who hadn't taken off a single bag for six or seven years, yet the soil was so good they got a bumper crop the following year and still came out ahead.

A waiting game, a man told her, leaning up at the bar passing the time. Got to take the long view out here, Mrs Russell.

Just imagine, she thought, if we'd got a decent crop, that seventh year at Rothesay. Just imagine if the hail had missed our place, or come two days later. We'd have got in that wonderful crop and it would have seemed foolish to go anywhere else. By now we'd be part of the furniture in Gunnedah.

Yes, and she knew she'd have gone mad. The seasons coming round like clockwork, drought following flood following drought, the only surprise the lack of surprise. Year after year the same, and seeing your children go on in the same rut, Frank and Max getting places of their own and growing wheat like their father, Nance marrying some local boy and having six children.

Frank and Max—well, they might have been happy enough. But she didn't think that kind of narrow life would have been enough for Nance, any more than it had been enough for her. They were alike in that way, she knew. It was part of why they rubbed each other up the wrong way.

Thank goodness for that hail, she thought. If we were still there, I'd always be wondering, who else could I have been? And who else might my children have become?

◆

Temora was a big enough town to have what they called a Superior Public School. It wasn't a high school, you still had to leave when you turned fourteen. But instead of all the children being in together, a Superior Public School had separate classes for the different grades, and the older pupils did advanced work.

She took the children along the first morning and was impressed. A substantial brick building, much bigger than the one at Currabubula, but the same pepper trees in the playground, and the familiar sound of the same bell when it was time to go in. The kids lined up tidily in their class groups, then the headmaster put his fiddle to his shoulder and played a march, one, two, one, two, and the children picked up their feet, left, right, left, right, and went in little blocks to their rooms.

Thinking of Eddie and his girls, Dolly considered sending Nance to the convent school, but the child made a fuss when she mentioned it. Shouted that she'd only go to school with Frank, had a fit of angry tears. It didn't seem worth another battle. She wasn't ten yet. The polish she might get from the nuns could wait.

At the Temora school they didn't have a star for the best pupil but they had a rubber stamp with a crown. Nance was quick at the work, got a crown most weeks. Dolly made a bit of a fuss when Nance came home with the crown, the way her own mother had when she'd come home with Mr Murray's felt star. *Oh, my clever little Dolly.* She tried to make Nance realise what a good thing it was to get the crown, but the schoolwork came easily to the girl so she didn't set much store by it, or by her mother's praise. She told Dolly one day, quite blunt and matter of fact, I'd just as soon it went to someone else, Mum. The boys don't like it when any of us girls get it.

After all their whingeing, the children had settled in, of course. At the weekends they loved to go out to the old diggings.

See, Dolly said one day when they came home with a few flecks of gold. Didn't I tell you you'd love it here?

Yes, Mum, Frank said, you were right as always.

She was startled by the grown-up mockery of that. How dare you speak to me like that, she started, but he was gone, off to show his father the gold.

✦

Dolly knew the children weren't interested in hearing about her family, but she couldn't seem to stop herself going over the old stories. Her father's humiliations. *You harbour the flies so.* What he'd done to her. *Over my dead body.* Minnie and the dead dream of pupil-teaching. The endless drudgery on the farm. The bloody yeast bottle.

The children fidgeted as she talked and didn't meet her eye, though they knew better than to say out loud what they were so obviously thinking. *Mum, we don't want to hear any of that*. But something drove her to tell those stories over and over. She didn't understand what it was, but there was some obscure feeling that in telling her children where she came from, she was showing them why she was the way she was.

And going over those old memories was a way to pick at the knot that was her feelings about her mother and father. She hadn't seen her father since the funeral, but she thought about her mother when she told the children those stories. She wished she'd had it out with her. Asked her straight up why she'd let her daughter go into marriage under false pretences. Was it, as she'd always thought, because she'd wanted so much to have Bert as her son-in-law? Or might it have been that she saw her daughter, still unmarried at twenty-eight, in danger of missing the boat altogether, with a bleak spinster future ahead of her?

She'd never know, only wished she'd asked, instead of burying her hurt.

✦

Having been a big place when the gold was on, Temora was full of Chinese families. They'd put down roots there, hardworking well-respected folk. Mr and Mrs Mee Ling had run the Man Sing store as long as anyone could remember, and Mrs Mee Ling could always suggest someone in her huge spread-out family when Dolly needed another maid or kitchen hand. She was a shrewd woman, never sent anyone too pretty.

The children were too old to need a nursemaid but with Max only six it was still a good idea to have someone keep an eye on them after school and at the weekends, when the pub was busiest. Dolly looked around for someone to help with the children and Mrs Mee Ling sent Sissy along.

Sissy was half Chinese, her mother was a white woman. She wasn't pretty, exactly, in Dolly's view she had too much Chinese in her face for that, but had a lovely warm smile. She was good with the children, seemed to really enjoy their company. She walked them to school in the morning and back in the afternoon, played with them after school, taught them euchre and canasta. Dolly would hear them laughing and shouting in the playroom upstairs. On fine afternoons Sissy would take them down to the reserve with a bat and ball and come back pink in the cheeks. Dolly joked she should have been getting married and having her own! Sissy just smiled. Probably had a nice boy tucked away somewhere for later, Dolly thought.

Dolly thought she'd never been happier than she was at the Queensland. Through her own drive and hard work she'd got them up the mountain and now they were sitting at the top, with plenty of money and the place in the world that money gave you. The Queensland was big enough that there was always some new project to keep things interesting, and with Sissy looking after the children, she and Bert could tour about whenever they wanted. To the lavish Cecil Hotel at Cronulla, a room overlooking the beach. To Kiandra in the Snowy Mountains, men slithering about on skis and the air so clean you could hardly breathe it.

At the Queensland she sat behind the till taking the money, in a kind of elegant cage of wrought iron, the gleaming zinc bar stretching away to one side, a subdued rumble of voices rising up to the high pressed-tin ceiling with its plaster roses and fluted glass lampshades.

She loved a length of red velvet and she'd found a good dressmaker. Miss Medway and her mother lived out on the edge of town in a little cottage, skew-whiff in one direction and the water tank skew-whiff in the other. The dusty road ran along almost under the front verandah, and out the back was a muddle of chookyard and woodpile and tumbledown laundry.

Dolly enjoyed those afternoons in the Medways' little front parlour with Miss Medway tweaking and pleating with her mouth full of pins. Mrs Medway always had biscuits for Nance, and Miss Medway took to the child and ran her up some pretty dresses, so Nance enjoyed the visits too. For once there was peace between mother and daughter. Dolly thought it was good for Nance to hear the talk about clothes. A woman didn't have many tools to shape her life with, but clothes were one. They told other people something about you: who you were, what you thought about yourself, what you wanted.

Miss Medway knew a few tricks to make the most of a woman, and did more than justice to the quality fabric Dolly could afford these days. There was a particular maroon velvet jacket. Loose at the bottom so it swung around her hips, a lovely floaty feeling, a little collar that you could turn up, very flattering, and a silver button at the throat. The first time she wore it, Bert looked at her with appreciation, went to the trouble of twinkling at her in the old way, and she let herself be twinkled at for once.

After twelve years of marriage they'd found some kind of companionship, sitting together over a drink in the evenings. In a pub you saw every kind of person the world made, the good drunks and the bad drunks and all manner of eccentric. There was always something to share a laugh about. She and Bert could get along on the surface well enough. When they were talking about the business, they could be warm with each other, not disagreeing about anything more serious than whether or not to put in underground water tanks or the new kind of gas heating.

He was drinking more these days. Whisky, he could afford the best now. But it left no mark on him. He was forty but as lean and strong as a twenty-year-old. *Virile*. She'd heard a woman in the Ladies' Lounge use the word one day, talking about some man or other. Kept saying it, louder than she had to—she'd put away a drink or two—as if it excited her. She wasn't talking about Bert. Still, there he was, a handsome *virile* man, and a woman married to a man like that was wise not to say no too often.

Once, when she'd had a glass more than usual, she tried to get under his surface. Asked him if he ever thought about the little girl he'd been paying support for all these years. She'd be thirteen now, just a few years older than Nance. Did she look like Nance? What if she and her mother, that Beth, came to Temora and she passed them on the street? Would she look at the child and recognise her as Bert's?

But when she tried to talk about it, his face showed nothing. Oh, he said, I don't look back.

She wanted more. Needled him to show her what was in his heart. Come on Bert, she said, you must think about her. Your own daughter!

Saying the words, thinking to jab him into revealing himself, pained her more than him. Imagining it, *his own daughter*, was like a knife turned against herself.

And he wouldn't rise to it.

I don't look back, Dolly. That was all he'd say. She let it go. Perhaps she'd rather keep it buried. She didn't want him peering into her heart, either. When you came right down to it, they'd always been strangers to each other, and perhaps that was the way both of them wanted it.

Letting it go. She hadn't known she could do that, take things as they came. But now, for the first time in her life, she'd wake up in the morning without restlessness eating away at her. She'd worked hard for that. She'd earned it.

✦

As she never had in Camden or Campbelltown, she threw herself into the social life of Temora. Perhaps, of all the places she'd been, this was the one that might turn out to be home. Dora Thwaites from the Criterion and Maggie Middleton from the King's Arms were in the golf club, and when they urged Dolly to come along with them it turned out she was good at it. She loved the feeling of whacking at the ball, the power of her eyes and hands and legs all working together, and seeing it soar into the air, sail off down the fairway and bounce onto the green. She watched the men playing for the club cup, could see how their shoulders and their feet were fighting each other as they swung at the ball. In her heart knew she'd have won the cup if women had been allowed to go in it.

She and Bert went to every charity do, all the dances and the concerts. Paid a lot of money to go along to see Melba when she came to town, couldn't believe that such a huge masterful sound could come out of that little slip of a person in emerald-green brocade, tiny on the stage. And there was the woman who took the photos for the Temora *Herald* and wrote up the gossip for the Women's Corner. She'd taken a photo of Frank in the school pageant. He'd looked very handsome as one of the Three Wise Men and Dolly went along to the paper for a proper print. There was Miss Norma St Leon, a bright brisk woman of Dolly's own age, bustling about with piles of photographs as if she owned the place.

Ah, the Queensland Hotel, she said. Very pleased to meet you, Mrs Russell.

Made a bit of conversation, was very obliging about the photo, and after that she came to the pub every once in a while. She'd pick a quiet time, order a gin-and-it in the Ladies' Lounge, invite Dolly to join her—only if you have the time, Mrs Russell, of course—and pump her for gossip. In return, Dolly noticed that the Queensland Hotel was often mentioned in the Woman's Corner. Its *gracious* Ladies' Lounge. Its *first-*

rate meals. Its *leading position* in the locality.

It was how men did it, Dolly thought. You liked each other well enough, but you were using each other. It was how you got on. Men had those clubs, the Masons and the Oddfellows and all the rest, where they scratched each other's backs. Women hadn't ever had any of that in days gone by, but here they were now, Mrs Russell and Miss St Leon, scratching each other's backs just like the men did.

She was a spinster, but not like all the other spinsters Dolly had known, creeping around poor and ashamed. You could see she didn't give a fig about not being married. As well as taking the photos for the paper, she had her own photographic business. She'd had a studio built at the side of her house—well made, set up like a professional's, no improvised hole in the corner. Everyone took their children along to her for a portrait. She liked children, and the warmth between her and them made her photos expressive and personal rather than the usual stiff formal picture where you could hardly recognise the child.

Yet she didn't strike Dolly as a woman hankering after children of her own. She strode around the place, bowling up to anything that looked good for a photo, nosing out any little thread of gossip, pushing you if you weren't sure. Oh, go on Mrs Russell, you know you want to tell me! She was a warm cheerful person, her life full of vigour and interest, unmistakably a happy woman. She had a place in the world that she gladly filled, and that was accepted by everyone.

Apart from Miss Murray with her little school, Norma St Leon was the first woman that Dolly had ever known who had

135

a paid job that wasn't about cooking or cleaning and minding children. Certainly the only woman she'd ever known who felt comfortable enough to go to a pub on her own.

You could tell from the way she spoke, her confident voice with the posh vowels, that she came from a wealthy family. That helped. But money on its own wasn't enough. To take up space in the world the way Miss St Leon did, you had to have some way of being out there in the full flow of life. You had to have proper work, the kind of work a man might do. Somewhere along the line Miss St Leon had learned how to take photographs and write up the flower show as if it was interesting. Knowing how to do those things was what allowed her to be the way she was.

Dolly took the children along to have their portraits done. Miss St Leon lined them up shortest to tallest, left to right, got them relaxed with a few jokes and the promise of lollies later. There was eight-year-old Max on one end, an open-faced lad in a new jacket looking pleased with everything, then Nance, eleven years old and pretty in one of the dresses Miss Medway had made, and there on the end was twelve-year-old Frank, the dark curls setting off his smiling face.

Musing over the photos later, Dolly was reminded of Bert's brother Allan, that good-looking boy who'd turned into a darkly handsome man. And Nance? Oh, what a lot of luck there was in life. With Frank's looks, Nance would have been an absolute stunner. As it was, the photo had caught her at a moment of excitement and happiness that brought out her beauty, but she'd never turn heads in the street, any more than Dolly herself ever had.

Would her life have been any different if she'd had those drop-dead looks that could catapult a woman out of a humble background into something glamorous? She didn't think so, not really. A beautiful woman might have a bigger choice of men. But she had to pick one, and whichever one she picked, she'd still end up a wife, with a life as small as the plainest Plain Jane's.

◆

As far as a man was concerned, a woman didn't have to be beautiful. It turned out that Sissy's warm smile was enough. And that she was convenient, downstairs in her little room near the kitchen. They probably did it there mostly, Dolly thought later, though it might have pleased Bert's secretive nature to find other places in the building. Danger a part of the pleasure, the risk of someone coming across you in some corner.

Which of course was what happened, Dolly coming back early one day from golf, and going to take the back staircase rather than the front, and there was a writhing darkness, a solid moving shadow in the little dark nook underneath where the stairs turned around. Really, she thought later, if Sissy's face hadn't glimmered palely out of that moving darkness she might just have gone on her way up the stairs. But there was the pale blur, and it was Sissy's face, and then there was another face twisting around, so there were two pale blurs in the corner under the stairs, and one was Sissy's and one was Bert's.

No one said anything. Sissy went past Dolly quickly,

looking away. Bert stayed in the shadow, fumbling around with himself, doing up the flies that hid that length of greedy flesh.

Dolly ran up to her room, slammed the door. Sat staring at her pale face in the dressing-table mirror. If I had a gun, she thought. She pictured it snug in her hand, pointing it at Sissy, pointing it at Bert.

Sissy. Sissy with her lovely smile and her calm warm way of saying, Oh yes, Mrs Russell, and all the time knowing the feel of Bert's thing inside her. Going off with the children in the morning, Nance holding one hand, Max the other, Frank walking along beside them, joined by their connection with Bert, a little family that had no place for her.

But she couldn't be angry at Sissy, not really. It wasn't Sissy's fault. It was the oldest story in the world, the woman who wasn't able to say no when her employer caught her eye. Dolly would get rid of her, of course, never wanted to see her face again. Sent a note down, she was to be off the premises by teatime. But it wasn't about her. There'd be another girl. And another. And another after that.

She wanted to wipe him out of her mind, couldn't bear to think of him. Her husband. Oh, revolting! Ignored him when he came to her room, heard his knocking, a silly tentative tappity-tap.

She kept coming back to the image of the gun, the feel of the butt of the pistol in her hand and her finger pressing against the cool tongue of metal. If she had one she'd go downstairs and find them and shoot them. First Sissy, then Bert. Right in their chests, where their hearts lived.

Yes, she thought. But then I'd turn it around. Put it up to my head.

She'd been so pleased with Dolly Russell. Thought she'd finally got both hands on the levers of her life. Now the hatred for Bert and for Sissy was all mixed up with a hatred for herself, because it turned out that being so pleased with herself had no more substance than a puff of smoke. There was a terrible cold knowledge where there'd been blindness. Bert had betrayed her, but really it was that she'd betrayed herself. Dolly Russell had been one kind of person, going along with her life and her plans and wondering should it be the red velvet or the maroon. That Dolly Russell was dead. More than dead, because never real. A puff of person living in a puff of illusion.

Now she was getting her comeuppance. Too full of herself to see what was going on under her nose. Too stupid to go on taking care.

And, like the other time, the sharpest pain was humiliation. How many people in Temora had known, had been watching her smiling and laughing and not knowing? *Poor old Mrs Russell, she's got no idea.* She thought of the boys down in the bar, the maids, all the people she knew in the town, at the golf club. Miss St Leon, leaning towards her over the little table in the Ladies' Lounge, all warm interest and *tell me more.* Mrs Russell wouldn't be the only person she'd have pumped for gossip.

Bert wheedled and told her a hundred times he was sorry. He was a fool. He'd never forgive himself. Never do it again, God's truth, Dolly. She hardly listened. It wasn't that he was pretending. He *was* a fool, he *was* sorry. But of course it would happen again. It wasn't a matter of being sorry or making promises. It was that a man's lust after a woman was like a force of nature, the same as it was for a dog after a bitch. Not something you could stop. And where did that leave her? She had no power, only this one: to make his life a misery.

She made him sell the Queensland. They sold so quickly they didn't get what it was worth, but she didn't care. She never wanted to see the place ever again. Was consumed by a cold frenzy to get out of Temora. Every street and every person in it was tainted.

She found a place thirty miles further west, the Beckom Hotel. Of course it was him had to sign the lease but he didn't argue, just signed where the man pointed. Sheepish and shame-faced. Frightened of her, she could see, frightened of her iron silence, her resolve.

She went along to the Man Sing store to settle the account. Mrs Mee Ling didn't say anything, didn't ask anything. But knew, of course. Had probably known from the start. She gave Dolly a funny little Chinese paper fan. It was nothing, but Dolly knew what Mrs Mee Ling was saying: You have my sympathies, Mrs Russell.

She didn't want any sympathy. She didn't want people being nice to her and feeling sorry for her. *Poor old Dolly.*

◆

Beckom was only thirty miles west of Temora but it was at the other end of the scale. Just two streets and a railway siding, a dead-and-alive sort of place. The hotel had a verandah like the one at the Queensland, with the same iron lace, and a parapet with plaster flourishes out of the same mould as those at the Queensland. But it was half the size of the Queensland, one end of the verandah was a mess of rotting boards, and the iron lace was rusty, with a couple of panels missing. The Beckom Hotel was a worn-out parody of the glorious Queensland Hotel, and the pretentious flourishes only emphasised how neglected and shabby it was. That was why she'd picked it. Rub his nose in it, what he'd thrown away.

Not many travellers stayed in Beckom, so you didn't have to have rooms to rent. That meant you didn't have to have maids. And they didn't need a nursemaid, because Frank and Nance were staying in Temora so they could keep going to the good school there. Miss Medway and her mother had agreed to take Nance and Max as boarders, and Miss St Leon had taken a shine to Frank and was happy to have him with her for a time. Now it was just Bert and Dolly again, with a stifling misery between them.

A week after they'd moved, waking up in the dull country silence, her rage past, Dolly knew she'd made a wrong turn. Yes, she'd solved one problem. She'd got Bert away from Sissy. But she'd created another. Now she was stuck in this little nowhere town, alone with Bert. She was punishing him. Oh my very word yes. Trouble was, she was punishing herself too.

She sat on the rickety little verandah, watching a horse and cart clatter past into the emptiness of a long Beckom morning, and thought about the tangle she was in. Ten years had passed since she'd sat in the kitchen at Rothesay, knowing she had no option but to go on in a failed marriage. How different was it now? All the money they'd made was tied up in documents that had only Bert's name on them. Very few women had their names on licences or leases, and they were mostly widows carrying on their husband's business, grace and favour of the authorities. There'd never been any question of Dolly's name appearing on any of those documents.

Still, she didn't think Bert would stand in her way if she wanted half the money they'd made together. He'd grown up watching his mother suffer and struggle, unable to claim anything from the men who used her. That had shaped him. He had a lot of faults, but she didn't think he'd be part of that kind of injustice. If she wanted, she thought she could buy some little business or other, a shop or a boarding-house, let everyone think she was a widow.

But was that what she wanted? If you were Norma St Leon you could be a single woman and enjoy it, but there weren't many Norma St Leons in the world and she knew she wasn't one. She didn't know how you'd become that confident, competent person living a life as full and authoritative as a man's. She'd been married too long and her sense of who she was had been shaped too thoroughly as part of a couple. If Dolly Russell was a woman alone she would be an oddity, a sad case, a failure. *She couldn't keep him, you know.*

She had to face it: she wasn't going to leave Bert. I'm not brave enough, she thought. I don't have the strength of character.

And there were the children. She knew women nearly always lost them when they left their husbands, the courts taking the man's side. Even if that didn't happen, how would a mother and father share their family between them? She and the children weren't always close, but she couldn't imagine being separated from them.

Bert had been subdued ever since she'd caught him with Sissy. Almost meek. Something about her catching him, the way she'd actually seen him buttoning up his flies, and the way Sissy—poor blameless girl—was tossed out on her ear, had made him go quiet. It was as if the urgings of his greedy thing didn't live in the real world, where other people were affected. He'd floated in a kind of dream, a warm dream of lust that didn't see any consequences beyond its own pleasure. Now that dream had collided with cold facts. He'd had that silly smile on his face and followed where his thing led, not looking left or right, and it had got him here. This was what shame looked like: a man who'd been knocked sideways by himself and the craving he couldn't resist.

He'd never talked about leaving her, apart from that time at Rothesay, even though it would have been the easiest thing in the world for him to become a bachelor again. For a man it was simple, and anyway a man was never alone for long. But she thought there was something in Bert that made him want to be part of a marriage, part of a family. To stick it out. Did that come from growing up in that little house by the creek? Was he thinking of his own father, whoever he was? That man who'd stuck his thing in Mary Russell happily enough, but shot off like a rabbit when she told him he'd planted a baby? And was he thinking too of his stepfather Henry Newitt, a man with a soul big enough to travel further than the dream of quick lust, a man willing to take on a brood of children not his own and do right by them?

By the time the sun had moved around from the verandah, she'd decided. She'd go on being Mrs Russell, part of that thing called a marriage. But she'd do it on her own terms. Bert was driven to get his end in. To try to stop that drive was to doom yourself to failure, grief, humiliation. The only way around it was to set things up so it couldn't hurt you.

Now, while Bert was still sorry for what he'd done, was the moment to get the three things she wanted. One was, never to share a bed with him again. Not once a week, not once a month. Not ever. Two was to own property, in her own name, that could never be taken away from her: to make sure she'd always have the choice to leave if she wanted. And three, she wanted to get out of these little country places where everyone knew all your business. She wanted the life and anonymity of the city.

1924

A Machine for Making Money

NEWTOWN was one of the worst of Sydney's slums, all poor people in poky cramped houses jammed into narrow streets. The Botany View Hotel was a stone's throw from the big brickworks and as soon as Dolly saw the advertisement she knew it was the one. There'd be no house trade, no night work. Just a lot of thirsty men coming in from the brickworks at knock-off and swilling down as much as they could before closing time. Not many on staff. Certainly no girls. Just a few barmen to slop out the beer and hose the place out later.

Until now she'd wanted the grand, the beautiful. It was time for something else. The Botany View would be a machine for making a lot of money quickly, and that was her ticket to whatever lay ahead of her. She couldn't see what that would be, exactly, but she knew that she'd be best off if she had plenty of money.

Frank watched her coolly when she told him about the move. He wasn't a child any more, you could see the man he would become.

All right, Mum, he said. All right.

No more than that. Like his father, he could simply withhold himself from you.

Nance had changed: none of the old sulks and tantrums, just wariness and withdrawal. The Medways had their own ways of doing things, Dolly thought, and Nance might have got on the wrong side of them a few times. The only thing she said about the move was, Will we all be together, Mum? Something in her voice—frightened to ask the question, but needing so much to know that she asked in spite of the fear—gave Dolly a lurch of feeling, the kind of nasty shock you got when you realised you'd forgotten something, left it behind on the train and it was gone, lost forever. It was an awful feeling. She had the urge to smother it.

Oh, it'll be so much better, Nance, she said. You'll love it.

◆

The Botany View was a square ugly building on a corner of the main road through Newtown, with carts and trucks rumbling past all day and all night. The name was a kind of mockery. You'd have to go back a hundred years, before the brickworks and the houses, to have a view of Botany Bay. The whole downstairs was one enormous bar, open to King Street on one side and Darley Street on the other, a kind of cave with no purpose other than drinking, with a concrete floor and tiled walls for easy hosing out. It was a hard dirty unlovable place. There was a bitter satisfaction in its ugliness, as if it matched who she was now. She folded up the maroon velvet jacket and put it away with a feeling like poison in her throat, somewhere between grief and anger. She'd loved that jacket. She'd never wear it again.

By six o'clock every day the place was roaring, a great crowd of men covered with brick dust getting in as many drinks as they could before Bert called time, spilling out onto the pavement, shouting and gulping the beer. The money flowed in as fast as the beer flowed down their gullets.

She took her time looking for a good property she could buy for herself and it was worth the wait: a block of flats right in the heart of the city, in Roslyn Street, Kings Cross, opposite the hospital. They cleared thirty pounds a week, and in that part of the city she'd never be scratching round for tenants. In the back of her mind, too, was the knowledge that she could live in one of them if ever she needed to.

She had to keep getting the deed out and looking at her name there. *Sarah Catherine Russell*. That was a person new to her. Not Mrs Bert Russell. Not even Dolly Russell. Sarah Catherine Russell, property owner and landlady.

Once the rents started to accumulate in her own bank account—in her own name!—she couldn't believe how good it made her feel. Anytime Bert wanted to walk out, he bloody well could. Anytime she wanted to walk out, she bloody well could too. She was forty-three. For forty-three years she'd been forced to accept the shape that men made of her life. The rest of the years, however many there'd be—they'd be hers.

✦

Max was only nine, he'd be all right at Newtown Public for the time being. But Frank was thirteen, Nance twelve, and it was time to think about what came next for them.

Times had changed. You didn't have to leave school at fourteen, the way she and Bert had. They'd gone a long way on that little bit of learning. Imagine, she thought, what they might have done if they'd been able to go further. She wanted her children to have that chance: to go to high school. She didn't know exactly what more you got at a high school, but she was going to make sure her children got it.

She wanted Frank to go to Newington College. It was where the judges and the rich graziers sent their sons, but it was also where that stout redhead from Wahroonga had sent her boy.

Dolly knew Frank was bright. He could do better than run a pub. At Newington he'd get a good education and he'd meet the right people, people who'd be useful later on. The school wasn't far from Newtown but it would be best to send him as a boarder, that way he'd learn more. *Pick up a bit of polish* was how Mrs Turner had put it, and she was right: it wasn't just about Shakespeare and Latin, not even just about how to hold your knife and fork. It was about the right way to hold yourself, that smooth confident way those people had.

But Bert wouldn't come at it. That's not our world, Dolly, he kept saying. Best stick to our own.

She knew he was right. Newington wasn't their world and it wasn't Frank's world. This was too big a leap. But they'd been arguing for too long, she wasn't going to back down now, and why shouldn't their boy have the best? The more he pushed back, the more she nagged. She heard herself, shrill, hard, hammering away at him with words like *opportunity*. Finally she shouted, You bloody pig in the manger, you don't want Frank getting something you didn't!

That jolted him. She saw his face change. She was sorry then that she'd said it, because it wasn't true, she'd just said it to win the argument.

All right Dolly, he said. Have it your way.

Turned away, as if arguing was a kind of intimacy, one that he was refusing her.

When they told Frank, his reserve broke open for once. I can't go there, he said. That's for the bloody snobs! Don't make me, Mum! Please!

She'd never heard him beg before.

It's such an opportunity, Frank, she said, but he cut across her.

Dad, come on, he said. Don't make me.

Bert didn't look at him. Best do as your mother wants, he said. You'll be all right, son.

But took Frank's shoulder in his big hand and pressed it. The two of them together on one side, her on the other. She was on her own with her triumph. And had she made a mistake? It was the dark side of having power: a little stain of shame, and of doubt.

You can be a weekly boarder, Frank, she said. Come home at the weekends. You'll love it, you'll see.

Even if Newington didn't work out for Frank, he'd be all right. A boy could turn his hand to plenty of things to make a living. But a girl was stuck on the flypaper of being dependent on a man unless she could support herself. And there was something else too, something beyond the nuts-and-bolts: it was about not being trapped in a world of small thinking that was all most women had access to. They'd never been told they could do anything bigger, and they'd been blocked if they tried. Finally, like a broken-in horse, they'd forgotten their real natures. They'd gone on and made a life out of the tame things they were allowed. Clever women, so many of them, but shrunken because they were women. Dolly wasn't going to let her daughter be limited to those narrow horizons. There were worlds of things to know and think about that she couldn't name, but she knew they were there. I'll never be easy with Nance, she thought. But I can do this for her. Give her the freedom I never had.

Oh, that lost dream of schoolteachering!

Frank was bright but Nance could run rings around him. Was that what made her such a difficult child? Always wanting to know why and why not, never taking no for an answer, having moods that Dolly couldn't work out.

A difficult child, but in moments of truthfulness Dolly could admit, yes, and I'm a difficult mother too. She recognised so much of herself in her daughter. Too clever for a girl and asserting her will too strongly. Seeing that echo of herself ought to have made her softer with Nance. Why did it go the other way? Why was she angry with Nance, when it was the world, and a woman's place in it, that she should be angry at? She was sorry every time she was sharp with the girl, but some deep well of disappointment poisoned the words as they came out of her mouth.

Newington had a sister school, Presbyterian Ladies' College, and Dolly thought about sending Nance there. But the private schools for girls weren't like the ones for boys. It wasn't about *the best education money can buy*. It was about shaping a woman who could keep the old-money households going. How to dress nicely, how to be a gracious hostess, how to manage servants, how to produce children who'd carry on the line. That wasn't what she wanted for Nance.

Eddie's girls had done very well out of St Mary's at Gunnedah. Dulcie had got five Bs and two As in the Leaving Certificate. Dolly wasn't sure what that meant but Eddie said it was a remarkable result. And there was Phyllis, just a few years older than Nance, she'd be going to the Teachers' College in Sydney. Eddie and Ada were so proud of them both, and no wonder. Dolly thought, I want something like that for Nance.

Gunnedah was too far away, but Mrs Phillips, the publican of the Commercial in Temora, had sent her girls to Rosebank

Convent in Five Dock, a few suburbs away from Newtown, and so had the Baileys at the Royal Oak in Campbelltown. Dolly wrote to Mrs Phillips to ask her about Rosebank, and she wrote back that the place had done wonders for her girls, she couldn't praise it enough. When the exam lists came out in the paper Dolly looked, and yes, Rosebank was there, the girls getting in the honours lists for the Leaving Certificate.

And in the back of her mind, if she was honest, was a memory of those boys. Tom Connolly. Jim Murphy. There'd been some inner thing about them, a calm smiling quality. She wondered if it was because you knew you were going to heaven, and if you did anything wrong you could spill it out as you knelt behind the curtain in the dark box, and come out cleaned of every mistake. That would give you a different view of the world. Not that she wanted to *turn*, or for her daughter to join the Catholics. But it was the world that had made those two men, and it had made them well.

Nance would have heard the rows about Frank and Newington. When Dolly told her she'd be going to Rosebank, she must have realised there was no point making a fuss.

So I'll be home at the weekends, she said. Like Frank.

No, Nance, Dolly said. You'll be a term boarder.

The blood left the child's face.

Only come home for the holidays, you mean? Oh no, Mum, I want to be a weekly boarder! Why can't I, Mum?

There was that pitch of whine in her voice, the pitch of the victim, that Dolly hated.

That way you'll get the most out of the opportunity, Nance,

she said. She felt her mouth snapping out the hard edges of the word: *opportunity*.

We want the best for you, your father and me. There's no more to be said.

Nance went off to her room without another word. Again Dolly was left with her victory, but again there was a shadow over it. Of course it was true that being a term boarder would give Nance the most of what the convent had to offer. A parent knew better than a child what was best for the child.

Still, she couldn't get Nance's question out of her head: Will we all be together, Mum? That little quaver in her voice.

◆

She'd never talked to a nun until the day she went along to Rosebank to enrol Nance. The principal, the Mother Superior or whatever she was called, had pale papery skin, and with the starched wimple around her face she wasn't quite human, just a face floating without a body. That was the idea, Dolly supposed.

There was a huge Jesus hanging from the cross on the wall behind her, not a nice thing to have to look at every day, but the place was gleaming clean and there was a sense of cool order. The nun let her peek into the classroom that Nance would join, quiet and tidy, the girls sitting at desks with their hands together in front of them, all nicely dressed and neatly brushed.

Dolly could see that, compared to them, Nance looked a bit wild. It was always a battle to get her hair brushed of a

153

morning. Good luck to the nuns! You wouldn't argue with those pale faces in their wimples. They'd take Nance in hand and soon put her to rights in a way she'd never been able to do.

No doubt about it, though, those nuns were a peculiar lot. Nance's weekly letters were full of how strange it all was. At night in the dormitory, she told them, the girls had to put their nighties on and then get undressed underneath, so no one would see anything! Even though it was just all girls together! Nance said that if anyone saw anything it would be an Occasion of Sin.

Dolly didn't like to think about Nance there among them, day and night, a stranger among all the Catholics. So she made a fuss of her when she came home for the holidays. Got her to show off the French she was learning, gave her all her favourite things to eat, took her to the pantomime. And all the while tried to silence the small voice in her heart that told her she shouldn't be sending Nance away.

✦

With only Max to look after, life was straightforward at the Botany View. She and Bert made a good team. She did the ordering and the books and Bert looked after the bar. It was just as she'd thought: the easiest business in the world to run, and the money coming in hand over fist.

But six months down the track she was getting sick of the rooms over the pub, sick of the smell of beer and brickworks and sweaty men, the way the place stank of vomit and piss no matter how hard the boys hosed it down. So when Bert came to her with the idea of building a weekender somewhere, she let him talk. She could see he wanted her to want it and he'd thought about how to persuade her. Done the sums, had the figures all there on a bit of paper. Even found the perfect block of land.

Cronulla, Dolly, he said. Up on the headland, the bush at the back door, the sea on one side, Port Hacking on the other. The kids'll be in paradise.

The minute he started talking she knew it was a good idea. She'd never forgotten those ladies at Wahroonga with their weekend places. With a weekender you could keep the money coming in but get away from the city whenever you wanted. Cronulla—they'd been there for picnics in the school holidays, that must be what gave Bert the idea. A lovely place. Not much more than ten miles from Newtown, and easy to get to, but it was like being on another planet: a sweep of clean yellow beach on one side and a long quiet stretch of bay on the other, and in between, a headland that was all bush, flowers, rocks, tree-framed views of the sea.

It was usually her trying to talk him into something. She was enjoying being the one who had to be coaxed. She didn't need persuading, but she let him work at it. There was a gentleness, an eagerness in his manner as he drew a little map, laid out the money side of it, promised her she'd have a free hand to make the house just the way she wanted.

Maybe he thinks it'll be a fresh start, she thought. And you never know, maybe it will be.

She asked around and found a builder. After a lifetime of living with someone else's furniture and wallpaper, with nasty narrow stairs, and windows in the wrong place, what a wonderful thing to plan a home. A proper home, just the way you wanted.

Which was: a kitchen that got the morning sun and was big enough for a table. No need for a dining room. A verandah to the north, where you could get the sun, but with screens that you could move around to suit yourself when you wanted shade. She came up with the idea of shutters on wheels, sliding along on a track, so you could push and pull them as you wanted. The builder wasn't sure, he'd never seen such a thing, but she kept making sketches and finally he said he'd give it a whirl, Mrs Russell, obviously thinking, It's your money you're throwing away.

She loved the house when it was done. Waking up there with the magpies carolling away, the butcherbirds coming to be fed with their sweet jaunty whistle, the sun scattering through the leaves onto the wall making lovely lazy patterns: that beat waking in King Street. Until it was gone she didn't realise how the stink of beer had got into her nose so deeply over the years that she'd stopped smelling it.

At the end of the weekend it was hard to get on the train and go back to grim old Newtown. One Sunday evening, getting their things together to catch the train, Bert said, in the casual way that she knew meant he'd been thinking about it for a while, What say we retire, Dolly? Plenty of money in the bank, what are we doing still working in that dump?

She went on folding her cardigan and put it carefully in

the bag. It was a mad idea, they weren't even fifty. She'd never known anyone who'd retired, let alone at fifty. But he was right. They had plenty of money in the bank, plus they had this lovely house. She had the flats in Kings Cross. They'd worked hard every day of their lives. Worked hard, taken risks. This was their time to enjoy it.

She buckled up the bag, set it on the table. He was waiting, watching her.

Good idea, Bert, she said, as casual as he was. Why not?

She and Bert had weathered a great crisis in their lives. Now they'd washed up together here in this sweet place. They'd never been close. Never shared what was inside them. But in their peaceful house, with money behind them and not a worry in the world, all the hurts and anger of the past could fade. Had she forgiven him? It wasn't quite that. But the good thing about her restless nature, about always moving on, was that you could leave things behind. *Never look back*. Not such a bad rule to live by, after all.

✦

Something in Bert relaxed once they retired, and she realised that the pressure to keep things going financially must have hung over him. She'd always been confident of the rightness of every change they'd made, every new venture they'd risked, but she saw for the first time how Bert might have been haunted by the ghost of his childhood. For a person who'd known hunger, risk was frightening.

He had a garden, loved to be out there turning the soil over. Just sand, he'd say. Nothing but sand! He put all the vegetable scraps into it and got a man to bring dung from the stables at Randwick. It was a side of Bert she'd never seen, his pleasure at picking up a handful of dirt and seeing the worms wriggle out.

It turned out he liked cooking, too. That suited Dolly. She'd be happy never to see another saucepan. Every fortnight he'd get on the train to Anthony Hordern's Universal Providores in town and come back with expensive tinned and bottled things—caviar, truffles, things like that—his eyes alight with pleasure. What he really liked best was a plain lamb chop with potatoes. But she could see how, for the barefoot boy from Curra, buying rich people's food was a kind of sweet revenge.

Just as she had at Rothesay, she'd lie in bed in the mornings hearing him out in the kitchen. He'd be rumbling away to Max, getting him his breakfast, making his lunch to take to school. She'd stretch, then curl back under the bedclothes. She supposed you could say she was lazy. A bloody loafer was what her father had called her. Women were supposed to put up with all that dreary work, but why should they?

In Newtown she'd mated up with Merle Phillips from the Imperial and Delia Delaney and her daughter from the grocery up on Alice Street, and one or two others. They'd all go to the trots on a Wednesday afternoon, have a glass of beer and a chicken sandwich and lay a few bets, watching the horses running in that strange tortured upright way, and behind them the tiny man like a monkey whipping them on. Once you'd picked the horse you wanted you got your binoculars up and just for those few minutes it was as if it really mattered. You'd be screeching Go Lorna Doone! and Merle next to you would be making a huge roaring noise like something in pain, because try as she might Merle never picked a winner.

They had their photo taken one day, you could tell they'd all had a drink, just enough to make them happy, Millicent Adams playing the fool as usual, tweaking up her skirt and showing a big fat leg, all of them laughing away. Yes, they were middle-aged, every one of them too fat or too thin, the grey starting in their hair and the wrinkles starting round their eyes, and did they care? Not a bit. They only thought of all that nonsense—being a young thing worrying if you were pretty enough—to love being out of it.

Just being women together, that was a hoot. Still, they all had husbands, and on Saturday afternoons they'd go as couples to the Randwick races. Bert was at his best with a group, a cheerful booming sort of fellow. She could feel affection, even admiration, for him when he was the life of the party. The other women laughed along with him but she could see how careful he was never to glance at them too warmly.

They bought a car and Bert taught her to drive. She was the only woman she knew who could drive. Oh Dolly, you're so clever, they said. She tried to tell them it was easy once you got the hang of it, but she could see that they believed what they'd always been told, that anything to do with machines was men's business. That was why she'd never really share everything with these women. They were still willing to go along with all that.

Other husbands might have been embarrassed to have a wife who drove. Would have felt shamed, as her father would have felt shamed by having a daughter *go out to work*. Bert was different from other men that way. He was pleased when she wanted to know how to drive, taught her patiently and was proud of what a good driver she was. Mind you, if it was the two of them in the car it would always be him in the driver's seat.

Oh, she loved that Fiat! During the day when the house was too silent, what bliss it was to grab her handbag, put on her coat, get in the car and drive off. It was the going, it was the freedom to go, it was the movement along the road: it satisfied the restlessness, the way a meal satisfied hunger.

◆

Bert might have got up mischief when he was in town. She watched him get spruced up and thought, Yes, why wouldn't he? There was a calm about him, a smiling care as he got the handkerchief just right in his breastpocket, that showed more than the anticipation of buying another jar of something foreign from Anthony Hordern's.

She turned her mind away. Rather some other woman than her. She didn't care, or not in any way she wanted to examine. After the years of pubs, where she'd forever been on the lookout for Bert fumbling away at some girl or other, it was a relief to be detached from all that. There were rows, but companiable times too. And she always came back to the same thing: she'd rather go on being a married woman, no matter how hollow the marriage was.

She was forty-five. The prime of life for a man, but on the downhill slope for a woman. If Bert left there'd be no other man for her. No one to shop and do the garden, and no one to be the man of the house in those hundreds of small ways a married woman comes to depend on. When the children grew up and left home, no husband to share whatever old age might bring.

She could see what it would be like, on her own in the lovely house, day after day, Bert gone and the children off with their own lives. As a woman on her own she could still go to the trots with Merle and Delia and have a few laughs. But a woman separated or divorced had failed in some way that made other women uneasy. She was a reminder of how fragile their own status was. A woman on her own forced you to see what you'd rather not: that a woman's place in the world, her standing, the respect she commanded, didn't belong to her. It all came from her husband. Cut yourself off from him and the curtain fell away to show a pathetic naked powerless creature. She'd felt it herself: you wanted to keep a distance, as if a woman who *couldn't keep him* was damaged, and her failure might be catching.

No, she was happy enough to turn a blind eye. She and Bert never talked with each other about their lives, but they seemed to have arrived at an unspoken agreement. They'd jog along the way they were for the rest of their time.

✦

Ever since Frank had started at Newington, that already-quiet young man had withdrawn further into himself. He never wanted to talk about the school or his chums. Dolly had a feeling he mightn't have too many.

At lunch one Sunday he said out of the blue, Dad, what does it mean if they say you're someone that has to buy their own silver? Dolly didn't know, but Bert let out a great laugh, half amused, half angry.

Means you didn't inherit it from your father and grandfather, he said. Means you're a Johnny-come-lately. Never mind, son, you just remember you're as good as ever any of them.

Easy for Bert to say, Dolly thought. He wasn't the one who had to go back to school without his cheerful father beside him, alone with boys who made him feel small. Still, too late to change now. He'd be doing the Intermediate soon, and that was more schooling than anyone in her family had ever got. He'd thank her for it when he was older.

Nance had gone quiet too. For the first year she'd enjoyed entertaining them with the Catholic business, getting undressed under the nightie and all that. But as her second year went on, it seemed there was no more fun to be had out of strange Catholic ways.

Then one holiday, halfway through the first year of the high-school classes, she came back bursting with some pressure of feeling she wouldn't talk about.

What's the matter, Nance? Dolly asked her. For heaven's sake, what's got into you?

She didn't mean it to sound rough, but she could hear how

it did. How did you reach another person? She didn't know, could only think of her own mother stroking her hair and saying in that sad way, *My clever little Dolly*. But she sat there while Nance picked at her fingernails, and finally it all came out.

She was in trouble at school, she said. Dolly felt herself fire up to give her the rounds of the kitchen, all the money we're spending on you, Nance! But didn't get far before Nance spilled it out: the trouble was that she'd been asking the other girls to prove that God really did exist. The nuns said she was an agent of the Devil. Said she was sending girls to Hell.

It was like the cold slice of a knife, when you cut yourself picking it up too quickly, not looking. The sharp side of the Catholic business, the thing that had cut Dolly off from those boys she'd loved. How dare they, those damn nuns? Her own daughter made to feel like the Devil because she was clever enough to ask a few questions about God?

Bert was as angry as she was. He went to the school next day to tell them Nance was leaving. He'd just paid the new term's fees and wanted the money back, but the nuns—oh, the canny things!—had already banked the cheque.

But where should Nance go? Not another Catholic place, and not one of those snob private schools either.

When Dolly left school back in 1896, there were only seven government high schools in the whole of the state, but now they were building them as fast as they could lay the bricks, just the way they'd been building primary schools when Dolly was a child. Millicent Adams had a girl at the closest government high school, St George Girls' High at Kogarah, a couple of suburbs away, and she said it was top notch. She gave Dolly the school magazine to read. The girls were learning algebra, whatever that was exactly, and there was a photo of them dressed up in white sheets doing a play in Latin. Now that was remarkable—girls doing the same work as boys!

But there was a tone of something else in the magazine too, something anxious, something trying too hard. It was in all the sugary little drawings of pixies and the nice little poems about flowers. Dolly finally put her finger on that odd tone when she read a piece where a girl said that the students might be able to decline a Latin noun, but what was more important was that they were ready to make good homes for the sake of the nation. *The sake of the nation!* Dolly tried to put herself in the shoes of a clever girl who could write that twaddle. She could only imagine the girl was saying it because she knew she should. A boy could learn Latin and algebra as his birthright. A girl had to promise that education wouldn't make any difference to her, she'd still be the servant of men.

Just as in Dolly's day, you had to do an exam in the last year of primary school to get into a government high school. Nance hadn't done the exam because she'd been at the convent that year. Oh no, Millicent said, St George Girls' will never make an exception, they're that strict about it.

But Dolly wasn't going to give up that easily. Seeing the school magazine had opened her eyes to what a girl could do now, even if she did have to go on paying lip service to all the old stuff. She was going to make sure Nance got into St

George, whatever it took. The principal, the person who had to be talked around, was a woman. That would have been unheard of in her day! But it gave Dolly the idea of sending Bert along to sweet-talk her. After all, if you had to be married to a man with a twinkle, you might as well get some good out of it.

He came home triumphant—there was a place for Nance, after all—and that night around the dinner table he made a funny story out of it, how he'd charmed Miss Barnes.

One of those spinster schoolmarms, he said. A bit susceptible, you know, to a man coming along.

Max laughed, Nance laughed, even Frank smiled at the picture of handsome virile Bert reducing a *spinster schoolmarm* to blushes and titters. Dolly felt the rage she'd been feeling for years, for her whole life. Spinster schoolmarm! She'd be some clever woman, would have started as a pupil-teacher, worked her way up. Probably loved being a teacher, the way Dolly Maunder would have loved it. Loved some fellow too, no doubt, somewhere along the line, because that was the way people were made. But if she'd married him she would have had to stop teaching, because jobs had to be kept for the breadwinner. She could feel it in her own heart, the grief that would be. Bad enough not to have even got to the starting line. Even worse to get started in the race and then be yanked out because you wanted to get married and have a family, like other women. Why couldn't a woman have both, the way a man did? Oh, she was sick and tired of the whole hopeless trick of it all.

Oh, you bloody men, she said. You set it up so a woman

can't marry if she wants to be a teacher, then bust a gut laughing because she's a spinster. Tails you win, heads I lose.

The faces around the table closed down. She'd been the cranky one again, the bitter one. The one who spoiled the fun.

I'd have liked to be a schoolteacher, you know, Nance, she said. Forcing herself to sound quiet and calm, so Nance might listen. But I never had the opportunity.

Over my dead body. She could still feel the heaviness, the solid cold rock of her father's will set against her.

You're a lucky girl, having the opportunity I never did.

Nance nodded, but Dolly knew she'd made it worse. As well as being the sourpuss who spoiled the fun, now she was putting a burden of obligation on Nance. All she'd meant was to open the girl's eyes to what was being offered. That was all, but somehow it had come out wrong.

But Nance might have been listening. Towards the end of the year she brought the school magazine home and handed it to Dolly open at the page where she'd got a mention. Dolly read it out. *A new girl, Nance Russell, joined us at midwinter, and is already proving herself one of our best scholars, having won the certificate for Botany.*

Good on you, Nance, she said, embracing her daughter. I'm so proud of you! She could feel her voice straining past the great swelling in her throat. It was love and pride, of course, but she could feel something else as well, a tangle of complicated feelings. There was something between them, like a splinter in the middle of the hug. It was that little long-lost Dolly Maunder who would have given anything to have the chance to be *one of our best scholars.*

She hugged Nance all the harder and in that moment Dolly knew how much she loved her daughter, no matter how shadowed and tangled that love was. Feeling her daughter hug her back, she knew that Nance loved her too, though in a way that was just as shadowed, just as knotty.

1927

Eighteen Thousand Pounds

THEY'D been retired a couple of years when Dolly woke up one morning with a different slant on her life, as if in the night her mind had turned a corner. She lay listening to the water down in the bay, the butcherbird that Bert fed, the white cockatoos screeching in their roosting tree up the street. Thought of the rest of her life here, stretching ahead, every day the same till she died. She was nearly forty-seven, and that was nearly fifty, and fifty was old.

Yes, the house was lovely, but too perfect in a way, there was nothing to take in hand and make better. She was getting sick of Bert being around all day, pottering in the garden. They were too much in each other's pockets. Theirs was one of those marriages that worked best when the two people didn't spend too much time together.

She had her friends, but to tell the truth she was sick of them. She knew them so well now, there wasn't a single thing they could say that would surprise her. She was sick of the trots, sick of the races. Wanted something. She couldn't put a name to it, but recognised the hunger that had been filled for a time and then come back: the old restlessness. It seemed to be dyed deep in the fabric of who she was, her need to keep moving. *Wanderlust.* When she'd heard that word for the first time she'd thought, Yes, that's what I've got. Lusting after moving on, finding the new in this wide old world. And enough other people had felt the same way for the thing to have been given a name. Once it had a name you could see that being made that way, with wanderlust in your nature, wasn't something wrong with you. It was just one more way of being a person.

So she found herself, as if idly, glancing again at those pages at the back of the *Herald.* The words leapt up at her: *Caledonian Hotel, Tamworth. Offered for the first time in sixty years.*

The Caledonian! Their wedding night, the feel of those lovely linen sheets, and the silk eiderdown with the embroidered stork. That carpet in the Bridal Suite! She could still feel the velvet of it under her feet. The week at the Cally had seemed like the seal on the contract: she and Bert making do with each other for the sake of a good life. Well, the making-do hadn't worked out all that well, but the good life had.

There was no better pub than the Caledonian. Dolly remembered how her father spoke about it, a mix of awe and scorn: it was four shillings to have a meal there when you could have a good feed at the Greeks' for ninepence.

Seeing the place in her mind's eye, she was back in that other air, dry and fragrant with gumtrees and clean country dust. Could feel the frost crunching under your feet on the grass in winter, the blast of heat in summer that scoured your lungs. The glorious emptiness of the air, the way every sound, every crow-call, was a clear single thing like a note of music. She hadn't realised she was missing it, but looking at the grainy picture on the newsprint, she knew it had been with her, a deep unheard call, during all those years of being in other places.

She and Bert had only been back to Curra a few times after they'd left Gunnedah. After the wedding or the christening it would be cups of tea and fruitcake and everyone agog to know Dolly's business. And how are you getting along, Dolly dear, they'd ask, and she knew they were thinking, *I wonder did she ever find out what Bert was up to?* They'd look at her shoes and her gloves, could tell that she and Bert were doing well, but there was always that put-down tone: Oh, a little grocery! Oh, Camden, now where's that, Dolly? Heavens, Newtown? Goodness me! And the last time it was, Retired! and she could see they were thinking, *They've gone bust and she's trying to put a good face on it. Poor old Dolly.*

She slid the paper across the table to Bert. Didn't say anything. He looked at the page for a long time. Smoothed his moustache, the way he did when he was mulling something over. Under the moustache he was smiling.

You reckon that'll show them, eh, Dolly, he said at last.

Let them see how well we've done?

A bit scornful, but she could see he was drawn to the idea. She thought he might have been as sick of being retired as she was. They had that in common, she thought, they didn't want to sit down twiddling their thumbs.

It would cost them eighteen thousand pounds to buy the Cally. Not just the lease and the licence: the freehold was for sale as well. If you bought it, every brick of that grand building would belong to you. But eighteen thousand was a huge amount. They didn't have anything like that in the bank.

They sat over the table totting up the numbers. If they sold the lease on the Botany View, sold the Cronulla house, dipped into their savings and borrowed against the Caledonian, they could raise the eighteen thousand. The only thing they'd hang onto would be the flats. That was important to Dolly. Those flats stood for her stature as herself, an independent woman.

It was a big thing, to go into debt. They'd never done that before, always paid cash. It was a risk, it was a lot of money to borrow. But there was no argument between them. They'd done well: the grocery, the boarding-house, the five hotels bought and sold. They'd taken a risk every time, and every time it had paid off. This was the moment to take one last risk. It was 1927, everything was booming, and they had the touch.

◆

Standing in the cool entrance hall of the Cally—the light from the coloured panes beside the front door making soft patches of red, of blue, of green on the walls, and a nice smell of beeswax everywhere—was a pleasure, but a pleasure touched with pain. She remembered herself there as a girl with Bert in their courting days, staring around in awe among a din of well-bred men shouting at each other in the bar and tinkling women leaving behind a waft of something expensive as they tripped past in their little shoes.

Old Mrs Trim had let the place go a bit, she was going on for a hundred when she died, so everywhere there were things Dolly could see you could improve. Not just re-furbishing, but making the place more go-ahead: for a start, the polo people needed garages for their flashy cars and you'd need to modernise the bathrooms. Then there was the bread-and-butter of the commercial travellers. You'd build some really good sample rooms out the back for them. Between the polo players and the tennis stars at one end, and the reps at the other, the place would never be empty.

They had to dip further into their savings to fit the place out properly, but once it was done it was magnificent. Together they nutted out the ad for the paper, got a man to take a photo. The angle he took it from, the place looked as long as an ocean liner.

One of the oldest hotels in the north and a landmark in Tamworth is the Caledonian or the 'Cally' as it been affectionately called by generations of citizens.

Business has been carried on at the present site for about seventy years, although the present 'Cally' has been remodelled and equipped in the modern style. It has long been a favourite house for district visitors and travellers. The bedrooms are roomy, hot and cold baths are installed, the cuisine is excellent, and the balcony offers a more extensive promenade than any other hotel in the north. There are 17 lock-up garages attached to the hotel, the present proprietor being Mr A. J. Russell, formerly of Temora, who has maintained its old-time high standards.

They'd agreed there was no need to mention the Botany View.

From the farms in the good country around Tamworth, wool and wheat poured through the town and made it rich, and the Cally was at the centre of it all. The old-money squatters came in from the big spreads, had the four-shilling lunch and spent the rest of the afternoon with gin-and-it and champagne before they settled down to a grand dinner with a baron of beef. The soft pink lampshades gleamed on the beautiful old furniture she remembered from being there as a wide-eyed girl from Curra: elegant glass-fronted bookcases, chaise-longues upholstered in silk, huge fireplaces in the public rooms with magnificent fire-dogs. People said that old Mrs Trim had had them specially imported from France. Oh, I wish I could take them home, you wouldn't think of parting with them, would you, Mrs Russell? the rich visitors would say, and what a pleasure to smile and shake her head.

The Kings were still riding high on the hog out at Goonoo Goonoo. It was the next generation on from the one that had humiliated Dolly's father, but the same family. *Stand back my man, you harbour the flies so!* In the season they had the polo out at their place, the clay-pigeon shooting, the croquet, the tennis. The King girls often came into town, shocking the locals with their hems up around their garters and smoking in the street. As they came in to spend the afternoon in the Ladies' Parlour they hardly glanced at Mrs Russell holding the door for them. There was a grim pleasure, knowing, even if they never would, that the daughter of the man their father had humiliated was now the owner of that grand place and every lovely chaise-longue and French fire-dog in it.

One Sunday she and Bert went for a drive in the Fiat and came back through Curra. What a dusty, silent, shabby little place it was. Being there was like squeezing yourself back into a bottle you'd managed to slither out of. They didn't stop. They'd done so well to get out, and now wasn't it good to be back, just to see what they'd left behind, and then head home to the Cally!

✦

Frank had done the Intermediate at Newington and got a middling-level pass. Bert and Dolly gave him a gold watch for getting the certificate, and Dolly hoped he'd go on and do the Leaving. Now that would be something! But all Frank wanted was to go on the land. When they'd bought the Cally he'd been as close to angry as she'd ever seen him.

Why don't we get a farm, Mum, he said. Not another

smelly pub full of drunks. Somewhere to put roots down. We've been on the move our whole lives.

That was true, and for a moment she could see it the way he did: never in one place long enough to be part of it, always the new kid at school, no sooner making friends than having to say goodbye to them. *Put roots down*. It was a way of looking at things that she'd never thought about. She'd had more than enough of roots, all those years at Forest Farm, and only now did she think how it might have been for her children. But Frank had his whole life ahead of him to do what he wanted. Hers was more than half over, and how could you knock back the once-in-a-lifetime chance to own the Cally?

So he didn't come to the pub with them, went to work on his Uncle Eddie's place outside Tamworth. A waste of that good education, Dolly thought, but she could see it was all he wanted, grubbing around on the farm, a shovel in his hand or on the back of a horse. And there was an obstinate streak in him. Like her own, she supposed. Well, a stint at Eddie's place might make him change his mind. And if not, it would make a farmer of him.

Max was twelve, high-school age. She wanted him to go to The Armidale School. It had been started way back for the squattocracy and it was where the old pastoral money had gone ever since. If you were in the know you called it TAS. Max wasn't a great one for the books so he'd probably only stay till the Intermediate, but she'd have given him the best possible start. Frank didn't seem to have got much out of a top school, but Dolly hoped Max would do better. He was more outgoing and sportier than Frank, more of a joiner, the kind of cheerful bloke everyone liked to have around.

Bert didn't argue this time, just said, Whatever you think, Dolly. Whatever you think.

He knows I'll nag till he says yes, she thought. He's just cutting out the middleman. She didn't like being a nag, but if you knew you were right, and nagging was the only way you could get it, what were you supposed to do?

Max went off in a fancy blazer and a straw boater at the start of 1928. Armidale was sixty miles away, too far to come home at the weekends, so he was a term boarder the way Nance had been at Rosebank. But he went off eagerly. He'd heard about the rugby they had there. And boxing, Mum! And a thing with swords, you've got to wear a mask over your face!

As for Nance, Eddie reminded Dolly again about the Gunnedah Convent where his girls had done so well. But Dolly thought that was yesterday's story. When Eddie's girls were growing up there'd been no alternative, but now there was: Tamworth High School, just a few years old, along there on Napier Street with something in Latin over the door. The government schools were just as good as the church ones these days, St George Girls' showed you that. And no need to deal with those damn nuns.

Nance started at Tamworth High in third year, the year of the Intermediate Certificate. She came third in the final exam, got prizes on Speech Day, a leather-bound copy of *Keats' Poetical Works* and *Poetical Works of Alfred, Lord Tennyson*. Dolly saw her up there in her white dress, shaking hands with the mayor, and thought, Well, she might be the girl, but she's the one with the brains. And Bert wasn't one of those men who thought a girl shouldn't be clever. He was as proud of Nance as Dolly was, clapping away, making a huge noise with his big hands, and there might even have been the glisten of a tear at the corner of his eye.

Dolly felt something rise up in her throat, something like a sob, a pain that she didn't know was still there after so long: the star that she'd got, week after week, at Currabubula Public, and the little poetry book—she hadn't thought of it for thirty years—that in her lonely grief she'd pushed out of sight behind the beam in the cowshed. If the rats hadn't eaten it, it would still be there. Now here she was, watching her daughter up on the stage, a young woman with a different future ahead of her.

The day after Speech Day, one of the teachers, Bill Crisp, came to see her at the Cally. He was awkward with her and she thought at first it was because he was so nicely spoken and gentlemanly and she was Dolly Russell who'd never gone past grade six. Turned out it was something else altogether. He thought Nance should go on to the Leaving, and he thought he'd have to talk Dolly into it.

I know there's a lot think education is wasted on a girl, he said. But it would be a tragedy if she didn't go on. Such a clever girl, a credit to you. You and your husband both.

She nearly laughed in his face, she didn't need flattery from some smooth-tongued teacher! She knew the Leaving opened all sorts of doors. You even needed it these days if you wanted to be a teacher. You had to get the Leaving and then go to the

Teachers' College, the old pupil-teacher thing was long gone.

But these days a girl didn't have to be a nurse or a teacher. A girl who had the Leaving could aim higher. Dolly didn't know exactly what aiming higher might mean, but whatever it was, she was going to get it for Nance.

If there'd been any doubt in her mind about Nance going on, Bill Crisp's visit clinched it. Not every day a teacher came and begged for a child to go on at school! She played hard to get, let him think it was his doing. That way he'd be more likely to keep an eye out for Nance.

But in Nance's next year Dolly started to see that Tamworth High wasn't the same as St George Girls'. It was the local farmers' kids who went there, and they didn't want the frills. There were no plays, no school magazine with poetry and high-flown essays. Only ten pupils were going on to the Leaving. No one at Tamworth High would have called themselves a *scholar* except as a joke.

There was another difference too, one that mattered more than knowing how to have a conversation in Latin: Tamworth High had boys and girls, but it was really just about the boys. Of the ten going on to the Leaving, there were only two girls, Nance and Una Dow. Dolly had to field many conversations about her daughter still being at school. What's the point, Dolly, when she'll just get married? It was a different argument from *Over my dead body*, but it came to the same thing: making sure a girl would always be dependent on a man for her bread and butter.

Bill Crisp aside, most of the teachers thought the same,

though they didn't say so outright. Nance came home in tears more than once because she knew she should have been top in some test, but the teacher had finagled things so she finished third or fourth.

Nothing's changed, Dolly thought. There were Nance and poor little Una Dow—it looked as though they had a better chance than she'd had herself, but men were going to keep on gripping their fists hard around the advantages the world had always given them. After a while a girl lost heart, fighting something so taken-for-granted. Dolly knew how that felt. She'd lost heart, and how could she have done anything else? For Nance there was no father saying *Over my dead body*. It was more hidden than that. But the upshot was the same: a girl funnelled into a smaller life than she deserved.

Nance had a bright laughing way with her, a sparkle that attracted the slow country boys at the school. And she liked being queen bee among them, who wouldn't? So she was happily drifting along, not thinking beyond the next tennis party, the next picnic out at the river. Drifting into marriage to one of those boys, Roy Axtens or Tom Fletcher. They were good-hearted young fellows, would make fine men. But their horizons were narrow. They'd each follow in their father's footsteps on the farm or in the little family business.

Dolly felt something like panic, seeing Nance drift smiling and laughing into a cramped small life. She'd wake up, of course, when she was locked into place by children, no other life open to her. She'd wonder how she'd let all her other possibilities slip through her fingers. But it would be too late.

The pharmacist Mr Morris was a regular at the Cally, often sat up in the lounge having a gasbag with Dolly, they both liked to follow the horses. Not quite a doctor, though everyone called him Dr Morris and the sign on his shop awning—*Medical Hall*—suggested it. He was a boy from the backblocks, he'd told her one day, his father a clerk in the mine at Greta. He'd had an uncle in the city he could stay with, so when he turned out to be bright he was sent off to Sydney Boys' High School.

Pharmacy, Mrs Russell, he said, it's the first rung on the professional ladder for a boy from nowhere.

Laughed, he was a cheerful man enjoying the success he'd made of his life. He was sending his son to Sydney Boys' too, wanted him to be a doctor, a real one. That was how it should happen, he said, each generation doing a bit better than the last.

He was a clever man, being a chemist. He'd opened the pharmacy the year before and it was already doing so well that he was going to open one in Manilla as well. He planned to have a whole chain of them, adding another whenever an opening came up.

So if you hear of anything, Mrs Russell, he said. I know a good publican has her ear to the ground.

Ah, that was why he came in and chatted about racehorses!

So Dolly picked his brains—what did he think they should do about their clever daughter who was doing the Leaving?

Well, Mrs Russell, he said, there's always teaching.

She could tell he was feeling his way, not wanting to be too definite in case he said the wrong thing.

Yes, Dolly said, but if she's a teacher, when she gets married she'll have to give it up.

Mr Morris heard the edge in her voice. She saw him decide to say what he thought.

Well, Mrs Russell, since you're asking, I might just mention that pharmacy has no marriage bar. And something else—it pays a woman the same as a man. Not many jobs you can say that of.

Oh yes, Dolly said, that's because the men who run things never thought there'd be any women doing it!

Mr Morris smiled, she could almost hear him thinking, Oh, Mrs Russell's a sour old thing.

You could be right, Mrs Russell, he said. The fact remains, a woman could make a fair living at it, if she had the brains, and she could have a family too, if she was so inclined.

The thing that tipped it for Dolly was that pharmacy was a business. It wasn't just a job, working for a salary. You'd never get on, working for someone else. The only way to get ahead was to have your own business. She and Bert were living proof of that. Pharmacy was a good money-spinner as a business, there was Morris doing very nicely. But it had standing as well, a step on the professional ladder.

It wasn't a degree, Mr Morris said, but you went to the university for the chemistry and the *Materia Medica*. The rest of the time you learned on the job as an apprentice. Dolly didn't have a clue what *Materia Medica* was, but what Mr Morris was laying out sounded right, a mix of the foreign and the familiar.

Bert was on her side. He liked the idea of his daughter becoming a pharmacist. The boys haven't got too much go in them, he said. Maybe the girl can make something of herself.

✦

At the Leaving, Nance got four Bs and something called a Lower Pass. That was enough to do Pharmacy. But Nance, that difficult child, said no. She'd already put her name down for the Teachers' College. Dolly wanted to hit her. The words rushed out unplanned. Over my dead body! she shouted. Over my dead body you'll be a teacher!

She heard the echo of her father's words all those years ago and felt a hollow shock to find herself using them against her daughter. But this was different. Teaching had been her only option, but Nance could have a different kind of future. She'd have a big bustling shop, people would call her Doctor Russell. Married or not, she'd be set for life. And here she was, acting as if it didn't matter. Couldn't she see how important it was?

It's that boy, she said. It's that Roy Axtens you're so keen on. What are you going to do, Nance, marry him and spend your life watching the sky for rain? When you could do so much better?

Nance stared at her with that stiff wooden gaze she put on when she wasn't going to budge. Stared and said nothing, as if her mother was a madwoman.

Dolly felt the familiar hot spurt of rage. You little fool,

she shouted, you can't see beyond the nose on your face, when there's a whole long life ahead of you, and by God I'm not going to see you waste it on Roy Axtens and a houseful of screaming kids!

Nance shouted back, All right Mum, I'll bloody do it, at least I'll get away from you!

＊

She was going to do the apprenticeship in Sydney, at a pharmacy in Enmore. Ten minutes' walk from the Botany View, wasn't life odd the way things came around. They all went to the station to see her off. Look after yourself, Nance, Dolly said, trying to catch her eye.

The words were silly, feeble, a thin pale little phrase trying to stand in for other words that she couldn't find. Words that would build a bridge to this young woman standing there on the platform with her smart little suitcase, the way she herself had stood on the platform at Currabubula all those years before, about to go off into her life. *Look after yourself*: what that really meant was *You are precious to me*, but the depth of her feeling was made shallow by the glib phrase.

She leaned towards her daughter, wanting to embrace her. Nance gave her a quick kiss but in the same movement turned away to say something to Frank. The kiss didn't quite reach Dolly's cheek. Then there was a great fluster, the train was starting, Nance turned and climbed into the carriage, everyone was shouting goodbye, good luck, bye bye, Nance!

The moment was gone. The past she'd shared with her daughter, the pushing and pulling against each other, was all there'd ever be now.

1929

Like Water Going Down a Plughole

IN October 1929, it was in all the papers. The stock market in America had crashed. Dolly didn't see that it would have anything to do with them, they didn't own any shares. But from one day to the next the busy Caledonian emptied out. It was like water going down the plughole of a bath, she thought, how quickly it happened. Not that their customers had shares either, but in the countries that had bought all that wheat and wool there was suddenly no money to buy what the Tamworth farms produced.

The graziers still came into town but they didn't have the three-course lunch at the Cally, they brought a sandwich from home and sat in the car to eat it. Went to the grocer's, bought what they couldn't do without, and went straight back. Out at Goonoo Goonoo the polo ponies were put out to grass, and those girls who'd shocked everyone by smoking in the street had to get jobs at David Jones. Even the commercial travellers stopped coming, because the shops weren't buying any new stock. Some great engine had stopped dead, and stuck between the teeth of its cogs were the Russells.

Between October 1929 and March 1930 Dolly couldn't escape a galloping sense of unreality. Every day there was some new bill she and Bert were suddenly not able to pay. Nothing like it had ever happened before. *Unprecedented* was the word everyone kept using till she was sick of it. The Russells had never had to scratch around to pay their bills, even in the worst days at Rothesay. Dolly had never, ever, had to go the long way round the block to avoid the butcher.

Things are on the up and up, people kept telling each other. Never you mind, Mrs Russell, you mark my words, things will be right again in a month.

But it was whistling in the wind. Dolly pored over the paper, trying to make sense of it, but the journalists seemed to be floundering as much everyone else. There were pieces about how it would all be over in a month and other pieces about how it was the end of capitalism. Were the communists right after all?

Eddie wrote to say he was happy to keep Frank on, but he was sorry, it would have to be just bed and board for the time being, no wages. There was no money for school fees so Max came home from TAS, brought a whole box of gilt statuettes he'd won for running, boxing, cricket. He'd had two years of good education, but it had been all about the sport for him. He told Dolly he was happy to get out of sitting for the Intermediate.

He'd grown out of all his home clothes so he had to go on wearing the TAS blazer. Forty shillings, she remembered paying for it not six months before, when spending forty shillings on a bit of wool with some fancy braiding had seemed perfectly normal. What was the dream? That world, or this new one, that you hoped you'd wake up from in a minute?

At least Nance was all right, finishing her apprenticeship at the Enmore Pharmacy in Sydney. People had to go on buying Bex powders and corn cures, and what she was paid just about covered her room and board at St Margaret's Hostel. She had to share with another girl and there was a lot of cabbage on the menu, she said, but she was safe and she wasn't going hungry.

Bert was a man in a stupor of bewilderment. He wouldn't talk about what was happening but flew into rages at trivial things, like his belt getting twisted so the buckle was the wrong way round. He ripped the whole thing out of the loops and flung it across the room. The buckle knocked over one of the little china geese, tinkling down in pieces to the floor, and Bert blundered out of the room holding up his pants with one hand and slamming the door with the other.

He was taking it personally, where she could see it was a matter of waiting out the bad time. It wasn't about them, it was everyone. She saw the photos in the paper of long lines of skinny men—women and children too—shuffling along in broken shoes waiting for a pannikin of watery soup. Silvertails, famous old families who'd always lived grand lives in Point Piper, were listed one after the other in the columns of the bankrupts. Not a single household, in the whole of Tamworth, in the whole of Australia, the whole of the world probably, was immune from the blight that had fallen over them.

The Cally was a Tooth and Company pub, and Tooth's gave them a few months' grace to pay their beer bills, but by February the tone of the letters attached to the accounts—all in red ink, she'd never seen such a thing before—was blunt. The day Tooth's told them there'd be no more beer till they paid their arrears, it was official: it was all over.

Bert just disappeared. Read the letter, put it on the table, went out and by teatime he hadn't come back. He might be up on Paradise Street, she was pretty sure there was a woman up there he was seeing, that Mrs Blake probably. Looking for consolation from her? Good luck with that, she thought bitterly.

Or he might have gone for good. It was what men were doing, just walking out the door. They couldn't stand not being able to provide. *On the wallaby*, they called it, as if there was something quaint about it, but there was nothing quaint about it. What about the families they left behind? Someone had to stay and listen to the hungry children crying. Men were supposed to be the strong ones, she thought. They looked strong and in some ways they were, but in a pinch it was the women, always, who kept things going.

She spent the day working out what she could do. The mortgage had to be paid every month but if she could scrape up enough for that, she'd get by. There was one thing she had plenty of: rooms with beds in them. People still needed a roof over their heads. She'd been a boarding-house landlady once before and she could do it again. Get Max out of that ridiculous blazer, he could do the heavy work, and she'd put the apron on and get back in the kitchen.

By the time Bert slipped in the back door and wolfed down the meal she put in front of him, she had it all worked out. She caught herself with a spurt of the old excitement—she had a plan, even in the middle of this nasty dream. But Bert wouldn't listen. Wouldn't look at the bits of paper where she'd done the sums. Wouldn't for a single moment consider the possibility of turning the Caledonian Hotel into what he called a dosshouse.

There's no shame in it, Bert, she said. It's not just us, it's everyone. Because she could see that was the thing for him: the shame. He'd come up from that barefoot world and he'd made sure everyone saw him riding high. How could he bear to fall?

I'd rather be dead, Dolly, he said. You go ahead. I won't have a bar of it.

And while she'd been doing the sums, he'd come up with a plan of his own. Which was, cut their losses in the pub, get a farm somewhere. You never go hungry on a farm, he said. And, unspoken, was his real thought: We can get away from here, where everyone knows us.

In May 1930 Bert surrendered the mortgage and Tooth's bought the stock-in-trade and the furniture. Four hundred pounds! It was an insult, a fraction of what it was worth. But surrendering the mortgage meant Bert wouldn't be officially declared a bankrupt, his name in those long lists in the back of the paper. In this hurtle into a chaos of ruin, avoiding that shame was the one thing keeping him upright. And Dolly had no choice. She might persuade and coax and shout, but it was his name on the licence and his name on the mortgage.

◆

She felt a great dry weariness when they got to the farm near Mittagong, south of Sydney, that was their home now. There were good farms in the area, but the one they could afford was a rocky ridge with a few poor sad skinny sheep skittering away from the car and about a million rabbits.

They'd only been able to get it because she'd found someone prepared to swap the flats in Kings Cross for this place. There was no other way to go on. Her tenants were all in arrears but you couldn't throw the poor devils out, and anyway no one else would be able to pay rent either.

But in the solicitor's office, signing the papers for the swap, she had to detach herself from what her hand was doing. She didn't want to have to feel anything. Just signed where the lawyer pointed, concentrated on keeping her hand steady.

She hadn't cried then, wasn't going to cry now, looking at these bleak picked-over paddocks. She'd done her best, had shaped her life the way she wanted it, made sure she'd be all right, no matter what Bert did. And now this thing, what they were calling the Depression, had come out of nowhere, a great spiteful hand that smacked her flat. Maybe you couldn't make things right if they weren't meant to be. You could do your best, but if life wanted to pull the rug out from under you it would find a way to do it. There was no point crying.

They sat silent in the car, looking out at the ramshackle house as if none of them wanted to believe this was where they had to get out and start their new lives. The engine ticked as it cooled, like a clock running down.

Plenty of bunny pie, anyway, Max said, a bit loud. Cheer up, Mum, we'll be all right.

That night, in the nasty lumpy bed with the kapok coming out, she felt as if she'd been holding her breath since the day in November the previous year when the phone had started to ring, people cancelling their bookings. She remembered putting the phone down and wondering what was happening. In her innocence she'd thought perhaps someone was putting it about that there were bedbugs at the Cally, was it those people at the Criterion? Every day another unbelievable bad thing had happened. They'd been sucked down into some dark chaos where there was no stopping and no turning back. Now they'd been spat out into this bleak new world, where everything she'd worked for was gone.

✦

In the morning Dolly woke up, seeing the light fall in an unfamiliar way on the ceiling, hearing magpies carolling.

Somewhere in the night the horror had left her. The worst of the horror had been in trying to push it away. Now the blow had fallen. It couldn't fall again. This was where they were, this was what they had, and there were things you could do, even in this extremity, to make things better. Get rid of those tattered curtains, for a start, and fix up the ceiling where the rat dirt from the roof space was falling out.

She could hear someone out in the kitchen. He coughed and she knew it was Frank. He'd got the fire going in the stove, had some bread frying. Turned from the pan to look at her warily. She knew he was thinking, How's Mum going to jump? Well, Mum was going to make the best of it, she felt like telling him. Just like she always had, and not look to anyone to help her.

They'd been supposed to leave everything at the Cally, every stick of furniture and every spoon. But who was going to know if they took a few things? Too many businesses were going bust for anyone to bother with an inventory. She'd sewn a few things up in blankets and hessian and sent them down to Mittagong on the train: a couple of chests of drawers, half a dozen chairs, the big oak table from the servants' dining room. Cutlery, dishes, a few pots and pans, bedlinen. If Mr Tooth wanted to come down to Mittagong and take the damn teaspoons, let him!

At the Cally, the beautiful mahogany chiffonier had held the Waterford champagne flutes. It looked awkward and oversized in this dark little kitchen, but it kept the rats out of the food. There was even a sad satisfaction in having those bits of beauty in this plain gaunt place, a few nice dishes to eat off, and the teaspoons with *Caledonian* engraved on the handles.

It had been her best effort in a hard time, finding them this place, and she knew it was up to her to get things going. Since they'd arrived, Bert had mostly just sat on the verandah smoothing his thigh with his hand, staring out at the dusty slope of the paddock, smoothing and smoothing as if to comfort himself. But she got him to work, didn't let up till he and the boys had the cottage waterproof and clean, had themselves organised with rabbit traps and a patch of vegetables, and were doing their best with the sad little flock of sheep that had come with the place. Bert had kept his old shears all this time—out of sentiment, not thinking he'd ever need to bend over a sheep with the blades again—but they came in handy now.

Max threw himself into it, nothing stopped him for long, and Dolly worked well with Frank. He had Bert's quiet quality, but it was mixed in with her drive to make things better. She liked nutting problems out with him, talking over the pros and cons—would it be worth swapping a few sheep for a milking cow? Worth putting in a paddock of spuds, or would there be no one with the money to buy them?

Frank was careful with her, didn't joke around the way Max did, but the two of them found a new companionship. Mittagong was a miserable place and their lives there were a matter of getting through each week waiting for something to change, but at least she and Frank had found a way to get on with each other.

It wasn't long after they got to Mittagong that Dolly's father suddenly got very sick. It was all over too quickly for Dolly to go up to see him before he died, and she wasn't sorry for that. There was a story that people told each other, that you loved your parents and they loved you, but perhaps it wasn't always true. Those deathbed reconciliations might work in a book, but they didn't happen in real life. At the funeral she thought about him—that harsh beginning at Goonoo Goonoo, who knows what hardships in London before that—and felt sorry for what he'd had to go through, but only in a distant way. It was if the Thomas Henry Maunder the minister kept naming was just someone she'd read about.

In his will she and Rose and Sophia were each left seven hundred pounds. It came in the nick of time, the old water tank had rusted through the week before and the roof was beyond repair. You could do without a lot of things, and you could cobble a lot of things together out of scraps, but you couldn't do without a water tank or a roof. She watched the men rolling the shiny new tank from the truck and heaving it up onto the stand. Thank you, she whispered behind her hand, and it rained that very night, enough to half-fill it, as if her father was helping her at last.

◆

Frank came to her one day, the newspaper in his hand. Look, Mum, he said, they're balloting land up in Queensland. Fifty pounds to go in the ballot and if you don't get the land you get your fifty pounds back.

She and Bert didn't have fifty pounds in the bank, nothing like it, but a week later he said casually, Oh, Nance was able to loan me that fifty quid, Mum, keep your fingers crossed.

Well, that was something. She couldn't muster up a stake for her boy, but on her tiny wage Nance could! A loving sister, she'd emptied her bankbook for Frank. I did the right thing, she thought, making her go into pharmacy.

He won forty-five acres at a place called Bringalily, west of Brisbane. The whole area had been overrun with prickly pear and everyone had walked off their leases, but now the caterpillar had got rid of the pear and the government was trying to get people back on the land. Fifty pounds down and the government loaned you the rest on easy terms. It was dairy country and Frank didn't want to keep cows, but it was land, it was a way forward, and he was going to take it. He went up that very week with a swag, couldn't wait to escape from the death-in-life of every day on those stony hopeless paddocks at Mittagong. Dolly and Max would join him if it looked all right. Bert would stay on till they saw how things went.

By the time she and Max got the train up to Bringalily, Frank had built a little place, not much more than a shed, but something to live in. He'd got a job with the council on the roads, spreading gravel, for ready cash. He hated being a labourer. When he joked about being *Frank Russell, champion gravel-spreader of Queensland!* she could hear the pain. It was a big day when he'd finally scraped the cash together to buy a few cows.

They were tyrants, Dolly thought, you had to milk them

dawn and dusk no matter what. But sweet-faced tyrants, with sweet natures. And even with a herd as small as Frank's, you could make a bit of money if you could keep the milk cool enough for the cream to be the top grade by the time you got it to the butter people. Frank had dug a dairy, half below ground level, and Dolly threw herself into the challenge of working out a system of hessian curtains and troughs of water to keep everything cool. It was like a war, she thought, the heat outside the enemy and herself the general who had to defeat it.

Some weeks she won, and the cream cheque was a good one, and other weeks she lost, and the piddling little cheque meant they'd worked hard for nothing. One day they found a dead mouse in the cream. That was a tragedy, a couple of days' work wasted. Dolly let herself have the thought, Would the butter people ever know? But she did the right thing and threw it all out.

There was always a new idea, a way to make things better, and two strong willing men to put the plan into action. And no Bert. No fuss, no drama, no big public split that she'd have to explain to every busybody. Just a practical arrangement, a temporary thing that could go on forever, one way of life sliding into another. Waiting at the siding for the cream train one day, she thought, I've never been happier, here with the boys.

Nance had some time off from the pharmacy, came up for a week. My word this is good, Mum, she said, looking at the hessian-and-water-trough arrangement. Ever thought of running the country? That was a good laugh, but the fact was, some days Dolly thought she *should* be running the country.

They made a go of the place, but milking cows wasn't what any of them wanted to spend the rest of their lives doing. Dairying's a mug's game, Frank said. Give me a sheep any day.

So when there was another ballot he went in it, and got land near Guyra, on the high plateau a hundred miles north of Tamworth. Good sheep country. He had to put a down payment on it, twenty per cent. Selling Bringalily would just about cover the deposit, but he'd have to take out a mortgage for the rest.

Bert came up for a visit to talk it over. Wouldn't hear of Frank taking out a mortgage. Didn't explain why, but they all knew it was the shame he could never name, of having borrowed and having come so close to having his name in those lists. The word *bankrupt* could never be said.

Frank didn't want to pressure him, but Dolly didn't hold back. All right Bert, she said. In that case you'll have to sell Mittagong and put the money into Guyra.

But he didn't want that either. What if Guyra didn't work out? Dolly could see that bad times either made a person shrink into themselves and turn their back on the world and its dangers, or it gave them the courage of having nothing to lose.

Come on Bert, she said. Tried to coax, when what she felt like doing was wringing his silly neck. We've had our turn. Time to help our boys now!

Why should she have to work so hard at persuading him, when she could see so clearly what should be done and how to do it? *Over my dead body.* She'd had no power then, and after all these years she still didn't.

It was Frank who was canny enough to work Bert around. In a dreamy way, just a man making pictures in the air, he talked about what size flock he'd start with. How the cold at Guyra would be good for the wool. How he knew a man near Guyra who'd got the blue ribbon at the Sydney Show for his fleece. How he'd heard the Falkiners at Haddon Rig would let you have a decent ram for a good price if you went about it the right way. Think of that, Dad, a Haddon Rig ram!

Clever Frank, Dolly thought, because it was the thought of the sheep that finally turned Bert around. Took him back to where he'd started, up in the shearing shed at Forest Farm, bending over beside her father, the sheep pinned under his knee and his strong right arm slicing the shears through the fleece, the wool falling away in creamy panels. He'd enjoyed playing mine host in all the pubs in his fancy waistcoat, drinking the best single malt, but when life scraped everything away, you turned back to what you knew, what you trusted, what had served you well.

◆

The Guyra property was among hills, a high tongue of land pushing out into a valley. It got the full brunt of the cold wind that funnelled up from further down. Bracing, Frank said, glancing at her sideways. What do you reckon, Mum? Not for sissies, eh.

He'd got a house up, one room, with a lean-to for the kitchen. But showed her how he'd left notches in the logs that were the floor plates, for when he'd be adding more rooms *as time goes on*. He used the phrase a lot. The place was windy and cold and, truth be told, not that good a piece of land. He could see that as well as she could, but *as time goes on* was a way of saying *there's a future here*.

There was a chook shed made of flattened tin he'd scavenged and a couple of kennels made of the same stuff. No wash house, just the water tank outside the back door and a chipped enamel basin, Frank's razor and strop hanging beside it, and his shaving-brush standing in a cup beside a cake of yellow soap under a bit of broken mirror. Looking at it that first day, seeing how he'd made his tidy domestic arrangements, she realised that her life had turned one of its corners, the kind you only recognised afterwards. That baby she'd pushed out of herself nearly thirty years ago was a man now, in his own private world that he was shaping the way he wanted. He'd make space for his mother, and his father too, but they were small unimportant figures out towards the edge of his life.

The three men were out in the paddocks all day. There was always too much to do. They had the sheep, so they needed fences and yards and shelter for lambing time. They needed hay for the winter and a shed to put it in. And a windbreak around the house, three dozen good holes, three dozen pine trees, little slips of things beating against the wind: somehow Frank found the time for that, even though it would be ten years before they'd give much shelter.

Dolly got the vegetable patch going, saw to the chooks, cooked and washed. Spread the newspaper on the table, there'd be no tablecloths till there was some cash, anyway what was the sense in things like tablecloths when newspaper did the job, and afterwards was good to get the fire going? Split the wood for the stove, she'd never had to do that back at Forest Farm and it wasn't woman's work, but the men had enough to do. She even knitted, she'd never wanted to sit and knit but they all needed plenty of warm socks, and as she knitted she remembered Rose showing her how, so patient with her baby sister. Dolly marvelled at the memory of that patience, something she knew she'd never had and never would, and thanked Rose for it, so that every sock was knitted up with a soft feeling.

Guyra was a bleak sort of place, the eternal wind nagging through the gaps in the walls, the great cold darkness shifting around restlessly outside all night, hard air streaming up the valley into your face all day while you chopped and lifted and stooped and carried. But it was home in a way Bringalily and Mittagong never had been. It was back to the climate she knew. Odd, she thought, how the weather of the place you grew up in got itself into your blood and bones and was always the weather you felt most yourself in.

✦

It was 1938. Things were finally looking up. The price of wool was still bad, though getting better, and Frank threw himself into breeding not just any old wool but top quality: fine wool. Dolly had thought he'd been making it up about getting a Haddon Rig ram, but there it was in the back of the truck one day. He couldn't have afforded it, only the Falkiners let him have it for a good price. It wasn't one of their very best but it was bargain enough to get started with improving the flock.

It was wearying for Dolly to be with Bert again. She'd forgotten how he filled the kitchen, how his mood filled the house. There was no escaping. Guyra was twenty miles away and there was no money for jaunts to town, only a quick trip in the truck to get the groceries once a fortnight. Nothing to see or do in Guyra anyway, it was even smaller than Curra, with something windswept about it, something empty and scoured and closed-down. She found something unsettling about the place, though she couldn't put her finger on it, and was always glad to head back home.

Bert hadn't wanted to bother with bringing the Cally furniture up from Mittagong. She thought he didn't like being reminded of that shame every time he went for the sugar. But she'd paid Herb Fanning to pack it all up and put it on the train. A rat had eaten through the back of the mahogany chiffonier to get at the food, but she loved having it again, loved stirring her tea with one of the silver teaspoons with *Caledonian* on the handle. There was some deep pleasure for her in having them, and the pleasure wasn't about owning a few bits of worn silver plate. It was because she'd rescued them. Everyone around her had dropped their bundle, and at that worst moment, she'd been the one to act. That restlessness in her had its bad side—she could never be quite happy with where she was. Distant fields were always greener for me, she thought. I could have that on my gravestone. The good side was this: she was never going to just lie down and take what life dished out. When things were at their worst, she didn't moan about it. She just found another distant field.

She cleaned out the chiffonier and got Max to patch up the hole at the back—those rats had eaten right through half an inch of wood! You had to admire them. Like her, they weren't going to give up, not if they thought there was something better on the other side.

1939

All That Claptrap

MAX was down at Mittagong, paying a visit to a girl he was sweet on, when the war started. August 1939. Remembering the first war made Dolly feel very old. She'd been in her thirties then. Now she was nearly sixty. They'd been at Rothesay when it started and it had been too distant to be quite real for the Russells. This war was different. You could see and hear it in all those newsreels of the man with the moustache pounding his fist up and down, and the great crowds listening to him, massed and frightening like insects, flinging their arms out in unison and roaring in vast inhuman waves of sound.

They were expecting Max back any day, but he wrote to say he'd enlisted. He was already on his way to Sydney for training.

Oh, her little boy, in some nasty tent out at the Sydney Showground, learning how to shoot people rather than rabbits! She'd thought about going down to Mittagong with him, just for a change of scene. If she'd been there, she'd have been able to stop him. You coward, she thought. You knew I'd try to talk you out of it. Rage and regret and helplessness, there they were again, the poisons that tainted every turn of her life.

But his letter was jaunty and she realised she wouldn't have stopped him for long. He probably thought it would be a great adventure. At the speech days at TAS it was always some bigshot in the army that gave the address, all that claptrap about King and Country. Boys loved a hero. Never mind that it wasn't much fun being a dead hero.

There was a parade in Sydney to see them off. She and Bert went down on the train and cheered with everyone else. Sergeant Russell looked handsome in his uniform and everyone was sure it was all going to be over quickly. At the wharf she waved her hanky at the ship, though the faces lining the rail were nothing more than pale specks under their hats and there was no way to know which one was Max. All around her women were crying and she found herself suddenly sobbing too. Bert folded her into his chest and for once she was glad of him, glad of his arms around her and him saying, He'll soon be back, Dolly. Never you mind, he'll soon be back!

Brave words, but she could feel the hand on her back trembling.

At Guyra they felt the gap with Max's cheery presence gone. They had the wireless on all day, a voice in the house that wasn't one of theirs. Dolly was glad there was so much to do, welcomed all the hard work, went at it from breakfast to bedtime so that she could fall into darkness as soon as her head touched the pillow.

They got a few notes from him, somewhere in the Middle East. They weren't allowed to say where they were. Dolly felt it every day, a weight on her chest as if she couldn't catch her breath, the horror of her boy on the other side of the world being—what? Shot? Run over by a tank? Face down in the sand calling for her with his last breath?

She'd wake up in the middle of the night and toss and turn. In the end she'd get up, go out to the kitchen and get the fire going for a cup of tea. She'd try not to wake the others but one night there was Frank padding out in his socks, rosy and cosy still from sleep. Frank, she said, and she saw him take it full in the face, her disappointment that it wasn't Max coming out to her. She hadn't meant it, but it had been there, and he'd heard it. He made the tea for her, brought a shawl for her shoulders.

I can't get him out of my mind, she said.

I know, Mum, he said.

He's going to get killed, while we sit here! Might already be lying dead. My dearest darling boy.

Frank threw another bit of wood into the stove, harder than he had to. Yes Mum, he said. Reckon we're all worrying.

She caught herself thinking, It should have been you who went off to war, Frank. She turned away from the thought, you weren't supposed to favour one child over another, but it somehow leaked out into the way she was with him, and the friendship they'd built during the hard years was withering under this new frost. She heard herself sliding the pointed tip of sharp remarks at him. It was her fear for Max, of course, but it came out as reproach.

Oh, that coward Ted Penrose, she might say. Sitting safe on his backside when the real men are out there getting shot at!

Yes, Mum, Frank would say, and she knew he'd heard the reproach. Turning the anguish about Max outwards, onto Frank—somehow there was the feeling that it would help, but it didn't. Every time she was sorry once the words were said, but she couldn't seem to stop herself.

One day in August 1941 Frank told them he was taking the truck in to Tamworth. Dolly didn't ask why, thought bitterly how lucky he was, going off to Tamworth when Max was lying somewhere with sand in his mouth. Frank came back looking dark and inward. I've joined up, he said.

Oh no, Frank, she cried, but in the wildness of her denial was something else too. It was only for an instant and she squashed it as soon as she felt it, because it was very terrible. It was a kind of bargain or calculation: if Frank went to war, it meant Max would come back safe.

They all said goodbye at the little Guyra station. She saw Bert's tears as he and Frank shook hands, and then shook again, and then shook once more for luck, the way men did. At least she could hug him. It wasn't something she and Frank often did, but she felt him hugging her back, and when he let go she couldn't see him through the blur of tears. It was an empty panicked feeling, watching him turn away and climb into the carriage.

The next thing they heard was from the army, Max had been in Crete, some awful business there Dolly had read about in the paper but couldn't make sense of, you knew they weren't telling you everything. Max had been mixed up in all that and then he'd been sent to Egypt. Somewhere along the line he'd got typhoid. He was being invalided home. Thank God.

She went to see him in the hospital. The typhoid had got into his spine somehow, he was in plaster from neck to knee. He was on the danger list, and it was shocking how thin and pale he was, but as soon as he saw her at the door he broke out in a big laugh, Oh Mum! Good to see you! And when he saw that she was crying, he gave her a wink. Those sawbones, they've got me dead and buried, Mum, but you mark my words, I'll be jumping around again in no time.

He met a girl while he was in the hospital, a nurse's aide. Was going to marry her, he said, as soon as this show was over. In the meantime, once he was out of hospital they put him on light duties out in the country at Bathurst. He wrote every week, dutiful letters full of nothing: trusting she was well, as he was, then a bit about the cold, a bit about hoping for some leave, a bit about whether it would be saveloys tonight or shepherd's pie, and then, the two small pages covered, he'd say, Well Mum there is no more news so I'll say cheerio for the time being, with lots of love from your loving son Max.

Oh, you dear boy, she thought, seeing his neat handwriting

on the envelope. Every week without fail, even though he's scratching round for something to fill the pages.

◆

It was ten years since Nance had left home. She was a successful professional woman now, pharmacist at the Coast Hospital in Sydney. It was where they sent the infectious cases, out of the city, on the edge of the sea. Quite safe, Nance assured her, she never went near the patients. And being a pharmacist in such an important hospital was a big step up from the little Enmore shop.

Then she wrote to say she'd met someone. Ken Gee, a funny sort of name. He was a solicitor. A professional man! Now that was better than Roy Axtens in Tamworth.

She and Bert went down to the wedding in Sydney. This Ken was a thin dark fellow with crinkly hair already starting to thin on top. He didn't have much to say to her or Bert, though he made an effort with Frank. Her son looked like a stranger in his uniform and there was no time to talk to him properly, he only had a half-day's leave.

Dolly thought Ken was a bit of a cold fish, to tell the truth, and the wedding was a stiff sort of affair, all very polite but not a lot of good cheer. That must be the way you did it in professional circles. Mr and Mrs Gee smiled and shook hands and they all stood there remarking on the weather, because what else could they find to talk about, these smooth city professional people and the half-educated folk from the backblocks?

Dolly watched Nance smiling and laughing with her in-laws and thought, This is what I wanted for her, a life different from mine.

Still, there was a knot of pain. She'd never really known that difficult daughter of hers, and now it was too late, she'd sailed off into her own foreign world. It was like watching Max's ship slide away, the ribbons breaking one by one.

Nance and Ken went to live in Maroubra. From there it was an easy tram ride to the Coast Hospital for Nance, and Ken rented a room nearby with a brass plate—*Kenneth Gee, Solicitor*—on the wall outside. When Nance found she was pregnant she kept on working as long as she could. She wrote to tell Dolly she'd have liked to stay longer, but once she started to show, the man in charge made her leave.

She went to the Women's Hospital in Paddington for the birth and Dolly travelled down from Guyra to visit. Christopher was a lusty good-looking baby and Nance was radiant. Ken smiled, but still didn't have much to say for himself. It turned out he was some kind of Communist, called what was happening the bosses' war and wouldn't go to fight. He'd left his legal practice and got a job as labourer on the waterfront. Dolly kept saying, But why on earth, Nance? Thinking she must have misunderstood. Nance finally explained. The labourer's job was because the waterfront was an exempt industry, and that meant he wouldn't have to go and fight.

Poor thing, Dolly could see she was embarrassed, even ashamed. After all, she had two brothers off doing their duty. But how could she go against him? She was stuck now she had the baby. Even if you had a profession, a baby tied a woman down.

She thought Nance's marriage probably didn't offer too much in the way of tenderness or understanding. That's how it was for me, she thought. It's how it was for my mother, and now for Nance too. Is there some law, that we repeat what our parents did? Never break out of that cycle of making the same mistakes, no matter how much we try?

Still, Nance was a happier mother than Dolly had ever been. She loved the little boy in a full-hearted way Dolly didn't think she'd ever quite loved any of hers. Her love for her own children had always been overlaid with bitterness by all the things that had been forced on her. Whereas Nance had chosen what she had. She'd chosen Ken. If you made a mistake in life, Dolly thought, perhaps it wasn't quite so bad if it was your own mistake, not one that other people had driven you into.

◆

Not long after the wedding Frank sent word that Sparrow Force—that was his group—was embarking the next day. Of course he couldn't say where they were being sent, he probably didn't even know, but he sent his love to everyone and don't let the thistles take over, Dad. A nothing sort of little letter really, but she read and re-read the few lines.

A few weeks later they heard that the Japanese had overrun Sparrow Force on Timor and they'd all been taken prisoner. Being a POW in a warm climate, well, she hoped that mightn't be too bad. She'd send comfort packages, like they did in Europe. Frank a POW, Max safe at Bathurst—at least they were both out of the line of fire.

But being alone with Bert in the silent house at Guyra, feeling the holes in the day where her boys should have been, was unbearable. While the sun was up it wasn't too bad, Bert was out in the paddocks while she kept busy in the house. The Clydesdales were his best friends, she thought sometimes, he was with them all day and treated them like kings when he brought them back at sunset, all the fussing about with brushing and blankets and oats. She'd hear him out in the stables murmuring as he fed them. There was a tenderness in his voice that she never heard at other times. But when darkness fell and he had to join her in the house, he was silent. She was, too. What was there to say?

The silence was full of Frank. She posted letters off to the War Department with *Please Forward* on the envelope, but she never knew if they were sent on. Timor, Java, Malaya, God only knew where he was. There were no replies. Then after a very long time a printed card arrived, a nasty little thing where all Frank was allowed to do was cross out the words that didn't apply and fill in some dotted lines.

Your mails and… are received with thanks. My health is good/ usual/poor/I am ill in hospital. I am working for pay/I am paid monthly salary. My best regards to Father, Max and Nance. Yours ever, Frank.

She turned it over and over but there was no consolation to be had from it. She could imagine Frank taking up the pen, no matter how unwell he might have been, and crossing out *I am ill in hospital.* But he left all the other options: *good/usual/poor.* That was to tell them that he wasn't tip-top but at least he wasn't in hospital. He'd crossed out the bit about having received mails. That was to tell them their letters weren't getting through. As for *working for monthly salary*! The Japs must think they were pretty stupid.

The *regards* were for *Father, Max and Nance.* But the card was addressed to her. Oh, Frank, you dear boy. She smoothed the cheap cardboard, where his hand had written her name on the front: Mrs A. J. Russell. His way of saying, I'm thinking of you, Mum. It's to your hand, your heart, that this message is being sent.

Over the next year they got two more of those cards, each the same. Then silence again.

The nights were long in the cold bedroom with the wind mournful in the trees. She knew she was dreaming about Frank. She'd wake up in the deepest part of the night and not remember the images or the sounds, but knew she'd been dreaming of him and there was no more sleep then, just a dark length of wakefulness full of fear and regret and longing. She told herself it would turn out all right, he'd come home safe and sound, and then she'd make sure to let him know how much she loved him.

Did he know she loved him? She'd play over in her mind all the times with him through his life, times that had been nothing but the onrush of the present when they happened. She ran through her memories looking for the moment when Frank would have known she loved him, and would be warming himself, wherever he was now, at the memory of his mother's love.

But every memory came back with a dreadful dark clarity and she recognised the blade in each one: the blade made by her, used by her. In daylight she could pretend that she'd been in a hurry that day, she'd had a headache, she hadn't meant anything bad. At three in the morning she couldn't escape knowing that she'd meant to hurt. Somehow she'd let all her own hurts be made into that weapon, and she'd turned it outwards: against Frank in particular, the baby of the time of betrayal. He'd grown a surface to deflect the blade, but eventually it had found a place to slip in. He'd enlisted rather than go on putting up with its cuts.

She tried to find hope, lying there in the dark. Drew the picture of the train pulling up at the station at Guyra, the carriages doing that little jerk, and there he'd be, thinner and older but still Frank, and he'd jump down and put his arm around her and they'd start again, all the hard years behind them.

She'd try to explain why it had always been so difficult. How some things had gone right in her life and some things had gone wrong, and how all that had shaped her into the person she was. How far back would she have to go, she thought. All the way to that night so many years ago when her father and mother had joined together in their bed? In that moment had she been made in the wrong way, so that she couldn't be happy with the life that other women were happy with? That she'd always wanted more, always had that restless sense of wanting something better around the corner?

She'd have to tell him about what had happened when he was a few months old and she'd gone out to the shed and decided to open an old tin trunk. Tell him too about the bitter grief and outrage of *Over my dead body*. How she and Jim Murphy had to torture themselves because of a few plaster saints, instead of growing old together, wearing into each other like a pair of shoes.

Finally she couldn't stand the silence and the endless tossing nights. She was over sixty. Her last years were trickling away on this windy farm, with this silent man, her children faint voices in the distance and regret eating at her. She made up her mind to leave. But where can I go, she thought. I've done the full circle. I started on that farm, with no money and nowhere to go, and I got free of it. Now here I am, back where I started.

There was just one way forward. Rose's husband had died and she and her children had taken the lease of a hotel in Walgett, way out in the dry country two hundred miles west of Tamworth. Dolly told Bert that her sister wasn't well and needed a hand. That wasn't a lie, though it wasn't why Dolly was going. But Bert didn't ask any questions. He'll be just as happy with the Clydesdales for company, she thought. After so many years, something between them had been worn down, used up, flattened out.

They didn't exactly say goodbye. They didn't need to make a big thing of it. Only, after thirty years roped together, they could go their own ways.

Rose had a bad tremor in her arm and seemed to be moving slowly and jerkily, like a bit of clockwork running down. Dolly's strong vigorous sister was getting on for seventy, and something was reducing her to a shuffling hunched person with an inward wooden look.

Dolly might have stayed on at Walgett for the rest of the war. It was good to feel useful and a release to be away from the stranglehold of the farm. But down in Sydney, Nance had had another little boy and Ken was no help at all. He'd stopped playing at being a worker and gone to join his father's legal practice, but reading between the lines of Nance's letter, it sounded as though his heart wasn't in it and there wasn't much money coming in. They'd moved to Mona Vale, in the far north of Sydney, the next suburb to Newport, where Dolly had been Mrs Russell of Beach House all those years ago. In the letter Nance said she had the idea of starting her own pharmacy at Newport. The closest one was miles away. She was sure a local chemist would do well.

Oh Nance, Dolly thought, a chip off the old block after all!

There was one problem: the children. Ken certainly wasn't about to stay home and look after them, and there was no one else who'd do it, no matter how well you paid them. Women didn't go out to work, let alone run their own businesses, and there was no one to look after the children of a woman who wanted to do that. Dolly remembered what it was like with little children: the ruthlessness of their need, the relentlessness of it. Nance's letter didn't exactly beg, but she had no one else who might help her out.

How the wheel turns, she thought as she sat on the bus to Mona Vale, seeing all the old landmarks pass one by one, each beautiful beach, each bushy headland. How would it have been if she'd stayed on at Beach House? This would have been her home for the last twenty-five years, the sound of the surf a background to every thought, the thick salt air in every breath she took, the bush forever tossing and glinting in the breeze off the ocean.

But she knew herself. She'd have wanted to keep moving, no matter how good a place was.

◆

Nance and her family were living in a cramped cottage on a long curving street with banana trees and palms that made it feel tropical. The area was cheap, and with houses in short supply during the war, it was the best they could find. Ken worked in the city, a long way to travel every day, so he often stayed in town during the week, and then it was just Dolly and Nance and the boys. Every morning Nance drove off to the pharmacy in her little blue car and Dolly was with the children all day, giving them their breakfast as Nance was leaving and their tea as she was coming home, and in between it was playing in the garden or going down to the beach, settling them for their naps, managing their quarrels.

Being a grandma was different from being a mother. There

was a closeness, but there was a distance too. You could love the children as the individuals they were, as themselves, as people in the making, rather than—as your own children were—part of the grain of your own past, with all its miseries and mistakes.

But it was awkward in the cottage with Ken. She didn't enjoy being his mother-in-law. He was polite enough, called her Mrs Russell even though she told him to call her Dolly, but sometimes she'd say something and under all the soft soap she could tell he was thinking what a silly ignorant old woman she was. She went to the hospital for X-rays for her cough, and when she came back cranky after a long day in waiting rooms she told them the X-rays had been a waste of time, she hadn't felt the heat of them. She saw the flicker of amusement in his eyes, he was laughing at her, though what was funny?

My own blessed fault, she thought. If I hadn't chivvied Nance into doing pharmacy, she'd have married Roy Axtens. He wouldn't have smirked at everything I said.

Though, when you thought about it, it mightn't be altogether about Ken. Being the third wheel in a household would never be really comfortable. Would she have wanted her own mother there every day, living in the same house with her?

Dolly was happy to help Nance and she liked being with the boys. But there was a sense of her life closing in around her again. What she really wanted was what she'd never had: to be a person on her own, free of any obligations, away from the great sticky tangle of family. To float wherever she liked, like those men in the Depression who'd turned their backs on everything and gone *on the wallaby*.

When Dolly told Nance she'd be leaving for a while, she didn't say anything. Just got that blank look on her face that she'd had as a girl when things didn't go the way she wanted. A barney would have been better. A bit of shouting would have cleared the air.

All right, Mum, she said. All right. I knew you wouldn't stay.

Oh, I'll be back, Dolly said. I have to get away, just for a while. You'll find someone to mind the boys for a spell.

She did go back, but never for good. She'd stay for a few months, leave again. That was no good to Nance. Dolly knew that. How could her daughter possibly run a business with two little boys underfoot, or leaving them—as she'd had to once—with a woman who shut them in a cupboard? She was letting Nance down.

But each time she left Mona Vale, marking off the beaches one by one as the bus took her down to Sydney, it was like climbing out from under a mattress: air, breath, a coming back to herself.

◆

With all the men away at the war, there was plenty of work for women, even an old half-educated one like Dolly. Her first job was in the kitchen at the Soldiers' Convalescent Home at Concord, not far from where Nance had been to school at Rosebank. She'd never had a paid job before but she worked out how you did it: looked at the ads in the paper, wrote a letter applying, and when the Home wrote back saying yes, could she start next week, she found a boarding-house near the hospital. Walked in the gate the first day wondering if she'd manage, was she too old for this?

But the work was easy and the big kitchen a warm companiable place, all the women sitting out the back smoking during their breaks, the fruit-boxes creaking under them as they chiacked with each other. No one asked anything personal. No one needed to ask where you'd been or where you thought you were going. No one asked about family. Who had a family so straightforward they wanted to talk about it? She supposed she should have been lonely, but she never was. Her life had become gloriously simple, as free as a bit of dandelion fluff among all these other untethered folk.

At the end of the week she got the first pay packet she'd ever had, a little buff envelope full of notes and heavy with coins. On the envelope, her name, *Sarah Russell*, and how many hours she'd worked, and how much money was inside. It wasn't about the money, though even an old woman peeling spuds earned a surprising amount. It was that she, without any help from anyone, had earned what it took to support herself, to go and buy whatever she liked, move from the boarding-house to another one if she felt like it, get on the bus and go into town, come and go without anyone asking what she was doing or why. All those years of answering to other people, all those years of arguing and scheming and, yes, she could say the word to herself, bullying, to make things go the way she knew they should—it was only now, when she had power over her own life, that she realised how strangled she'd been by not having it.

A thought took her by surprise: I should have been born a man. But that wasn't it. She didn't want to be a man. She just wanted to be a woman with the same freedom to choose that a man had.

Then Concord got a new manager, chivvied them to work harder and docked their pay if they were a minute late. What freedom, to walk away. She got another job the next day, in the kitchen at St Anne's Hospital. When she got tired of that she went to the canteen at Australasian Metalworkers.

The best job she had was at the posh Australia Hotel in the middle of the city, in charge of the women's toilet. She'd hand the towel to the ladies in their fur collars—as if they couldn't pick it up themselves!—but that was worth threepence in the saucer. Her real job, though, the reason the management paid her, was to keep people from coming in off the street and using the facilities. She'd seen the thought on the man's face when he'd interviewed her: *This old battleaxe will scare away the riffraff.*

✦

Dolly was back at Nance's place when the news everyone was waiting for came over the wireless: the war was over. Straightaway she sat down to write to Frank at the address on the last card they'd had from him: No. 4 POW Camp, Thailand.

Crescent Rd
Mona Vale

My dearest Son,

At last you are free. I thank Almighty God for your deliverance. I only hope you are as well as can be expected after the terrible years that you have gone through. We have read how bad things were but knew we could only hope and pray. We all long for the day when we will see your dear face once more. All are well here. Staying with Nancy at the above address. She has two lovely boys and is working at her profession & I am looking after the children. We all wrote often to you but I don't know if you got our letters. Just send us 2 lines to let us know when you will be home. You may be in hospital, but so long as we know, every day is nearer to our being together again. I gave up hope when I had no word for so long. I lived only till I could see you again my darling. The only way I could stop from going mental was by working. Everyone has constantly asked about you & been kind. Thank God we are still free here in Australia, it was very close to being invaded one time and can thank America for coming to the rescue. I've just heard they are dropping supplies to all those in the prison camps. Everybody sends love & greetings & messages they will also write as soon as we know.

Your loving mother
Nance is overjoyed & sends her warmest love to you.

Four days later the news came. Frank was dead. He'd died on the railway the Japanese had forced the POWs to build. He'd been dead for eighteen months. All that hope, all those warm thoughts sent from Dolly's mind to his, all that love: all wasted, empty. Worse than that, a mockery.

1945

Plus and Minus

DOLLY woke up every morning with Frank still alive, a warm presence with her in the room. Alive, and she was speaking to him, making all those promises about how the future would be different.

Then she remembered. There was no escape from the pain of it then. Not by sleeping, not by waking, not by working, not by walking, not by talking. There was only this one fact: Frank was dead.

Her letter to Frank came back, returned by the army. She couldn't bear to open it and read what she'd written in such hope, but she couldn't throw it away either. A few months later, a letter came from Department of the Army Concession, whatever that was. It had gone all around, re-addressed from Guyra to Walgett and finally to Mona Vale. Sender, Lt J. Carrick.

Lt J. Carrick turned out to be Frank's commanding officer, and the letter was short but kind. Lt Carrick was so very sorry, Russ was a good man, one of the best. Had always taken care of the other men, made sure they didn't let the flies land on their food, kept them going with jokes. He sent his most sincere condolences.

She treasured the letter, loved knowing the nickname his mates had called him by. *Russ.* Yes, he'd never liked the name Frank.

Then the medals came, each in its own little box with a bright striped ribbon folded neatly under the shiny metal. Looking at them, she was sickened. The waste, the waste. Were these little bits of rubbish supposed to make it better? Nance came in and found her with them in her hand. Put her arm around her mother and they stood silent together for a long stretch of time.

She found herself talking to strangers now on the bus and in shops, pouring it all out about Frank, as if telling the story would make it come out differently. Some woman she met at the Newport butcher's told her about a Mrs Baker, a bus ride away at Dee Why.

She went to Mrs Baker's half a dozen times. Bought the little magazine she sold, *The Harbinger of Light*, and sat with the woman in her fusty little front room with the antimacassars on the chintz armchairs and the china geese lined up along the mantelpiece. Mrs Baker would greet her, sit her down, draw the curtains against the afternoon light, stub out her cigarette and put a fringed shawl around her shoulders. Then she'd sit very still, close her eyes, sway around a bit, make noises in her throat. Are you receptive, dear, she'd murmur, and Dolly would murmur, Yes.

Was she receptive? Did she believe this woman could connect her with Frank? Or was it just somewhere to put the pain for a few minutes?

When Mrs Baker opened her eyes again they were fixed and starey, as if she was looking through the wall out to the horizon where the sea glittered. She'd make more noises, say a few words, and then she'd fumble, her many rings catching the light, for the pen and paper she'd got ready.

The few words didn't ever make much sense, but sometimes you could imagine a message. *Tender and true. Sit alone. Soldier boy.* Come back next week, dear, Mrs Baker would say at the end, when she was herself again, had taken off the shawl, lit another Craven A, and folded up the pound note.

I feel your dear boy drawing closer every time, don't you, dear? she'd say, and what could Dolly say but yes, and perhaps it was true. Had she felt something in that dim room, felt a rustle of spirit in her heart that might be Frank? She'd go home with the scrap of cheap lined paper with the few words scrawled on it, sleep with it under her pillow.

She didn't tell Nance. Certainly not Ken. She could imagine how his eyebrows would go up and his voice would get a bit silky. Oh, now that's interesting Mrs Russell, and what did Frank say exactly? She couldn't blame him. She'd have laughed at herself, but she'd do anything to ease the pain.

One afternoon she arrived at Mrs Baker's early, and as she reached the gate another woman was coming out. She was holding a sheet of that same lined paper, clutching it as if it was a diamond she was afraid of losing. The woman didn't see Dolly, went off down the street, just another old woman in a shabby brown coat that was a bit like her own.

Seeing herself like that, from the outside, shifted something in the feel of the afternoon. She went in and sat down and Mrs Baker dimmed the room and put the shawl on as usual, but Dolly knew Mrs Baker felt a difference in her. She went into the murmuring and the swaying, but there was something businesslike about the way she reached for the pen. This time she wrote half a page. It was a kind of poem about *A soldier boy to the war did go, fighting hard to beat the foe.* It ended: *When you sit alone I am with you Mother, just to whisper in your ear. Not goodbye just good night. Love Frank.*

Dolly had it folded up small in her handbag all the way home on the bus. It was the last time she'd go to Mrs Baker. The woman knew it too. She'd given her a shrewd look as they said goodbye.

When you sit alone I am with you Mother. She stared out the dirty window at the world passing, the shops, the palm trees along Pittwater Road, the people walking about, the seagulls wheeling and hanging in the afternoon sea breeze. Yes, Frank was with her. Not because of any woman murmuring and swaying and taking down dictation from the other side. But just because he would always be part of who she was, of all the things, good and bad, that had ever happened to her. From the day at Rothesay when she'd known she must be pregnant, right up to that moment on the station at Guyra, feeling his strong body hugging her, he'd been part of her life. Even later, when he'd thought whether to address the precious little card to his mother or his father, Frank was still joined to her.

Still with her. Not the same way Max was, married now and living out at Blacktown with a little boy of his own. And not the way Nance was, a brisk busy woman managing too many different things every day. But always with her.

They shall not grow old, as we that are left grow old. He'd always be that man of twenty-nine who'd said goodbye to her. Always be that man who'd only had a year of having his own farm, the thing he'd always wanted, before he went off to fight. He hadn't gone to defend any silly idea about King and Country—someone else's king, someone else's country—but his own little patch of the earth. And he'd gone because she'd made him. That could never be put right. She could never undo that, never be without the pain of it. But the pain joined her to him. While she felt that pain, Frank was still with her.

He'd addressed the cards to her. In the worst times, that was something to hang on to.

◆

Nance had a third child in 1950, a girl called Catherine. They'd moved from Mona Vale to a house in Alfred Street, North Sydney, just over the bridge from the city. The place had a

229

separate flat at the side, and Nance said it was Dolly's if ever she wanted it. She would, one of these days. Her cough was getting worse and she was weak as a kitten some mornings.

Nance knows me, she thought. Knows I need that free feeling, being able to come and go as I please. Most people seem to need other people around them, feel lonely if they're not part of a couple. I'm not like that. Maybe there's something wrong with me, or maybe something in those early days shaped me like that, but there it is. I'm happiest on my own. Nance knows that, and she's not going to judge me for it.

✦

The house had once been a grand place and the flat at the side had been the billiard room. Ken had built some partitions and put in a basic kitchen and bathroom. He'd done quite a neat job. He was a funny mixture of a man, Dolly thought: he was a bit of an intellectual, but at the same time he loved nothing better than pottering about with a hammer in his hand.

Dolly's bed was in an alcove, with a big fancy window behind it made of panes of coloured glass that reminded her of something. It took her a while to remember there'd been just the same panes of red, of blue, of green, around the ornate front door of the Caledonian Hotel in Tamworth. She sat in her armchair during the long afternoons, watching the coloured light—vague shapes like slow dim underwater creatures—travel slowly along the floor and up the wall, just as it had travelled around the wide entrance of the Cally. Back then she'd never had time to watch it. After a lifetime of restlessness, she was happy now to do nothing more than sit half-sleeping, half-musing, her thoughts floating about like the shapes on the wall.

When the sun slid down behind the roof next door and cut out the light from the coloured panes, she'd get up and make her way out to the garden outside her kitchen where Nance's children sometimes played.

She didn't seem to have the knack with children. Hadn't with her own, didn't with these three grandchildren either. Nance was too easy on them, it was the modern way of doing it, never say no to the child.

Dolly had roused on Stephen, the younger boy, one afternoon, for getting his pants all over mud, playing with his cars on the ground. Just a gentle rousing, but she could see the fear on his face. She hadn't wanted to frighten him, just wanted to throw a little lasso of words to the boy, and have him throw something back, and they'd go along from there. But what had come out was wrong. The sharpness was the habit of a lifetime. It was the voice she'd heard from her own mother, and it was the voice she'd learned to use herself when life treated her badly. But oh, was there no way to break that old pattern?

So when she came across the little one, the girl, one afternoon under the tall camellia in the corner, she bit back the scolding. The child stood looking up at her, dirt all over her face and her hair a tangle of curls with twigs caught in the strands. Frank's hair, she realised, and something of Frank in the child's face too. Thinking of all the soft words she'd never said, to Frank or anyone else, the question was out before she'd planned it: Do you love me, Cathy?

She'd never asked such a thing in her life. Never thought to ask it of Bert, never needed to ask it of Jim Murphy. It had never occurred to her to ask it of her children. But here it was, coming out of nowhere into the unsmiling face of this child she barely knew. Who thought about it, it seemed, then said *No*, just like that, and turned around as if it was nothing and went back out into the other part of the garden.

How dare she? Cheeky little miss, needs a good hiding! Dolly was still cranky when she saw Nance, gave her a piece of her mind about her rude daughter. Nance said she was sorry, she'd speak to Cathy about it.

But later, in bed that night, looking at the repeating pattern of the pressed-tin ceiling, block after block complicated but all the same, like the days of a life, she saw it differently. What a good thing that the child was able to say the truth, she thought. My generation always had to pretend. Of course she hadn't wanted to hear the truth. But if the child had said, Oh yes Grandma, I do love you, Dolly would have known she was only saying what she knew she should. That little girl lived in a different world from the one she'd grown up in. It was a better one, where a child had been taught that it was all right to say the truth.

There was a wry pleasure in knowing that her time was gone. She couldn't have it over again, was too weary now to even wish she could. She'd been unlucky, born in the place and time she had been. But she'd battled against that time and place, and that battle had something to do with this new world, where a girl could say what she truly thought.

She thought of all the women she'd ever known, and all their mothers before them, and the mothers before those mothers, locked into a place where they couldn't move. My generation was like the hinge, she thought. The door had been shut tight, and when it started to swing open, my generation was the hinge that it had to be forced around on, one surface grinding over another. No wonder it was painful.

She'd done a few things. Right things, wrong things. Things done that shouldn't have been done, and things not done when they should have been. There was no ledger where you could add it all up and come up with a number at the bottom, plus or minus. All you could say was, you were born into a world that made it easy for you or made it hard for you, and all you could do was stumble along under the weight of whatever you'd been given to carry. No wonder at the end of it you were tired, and sad. But glad to have done it all, even the mistakes. Glad to be alive, too. Even if you were only alive enough to watch another day's light slide along the wall, and wait for the night.

This is a portrait of Dolly Maunder, taken a few years before she married.

The dress, the chair, and the columns-and-stairs backdrop,
were all supplied by the photographer. Only her face is her own.

The photo was among my mother's papers when she died.
Dolly was her mother and my grandmother.

Grandma

NUMBER 302 Alfred Street, North Sydney, where I spent my childhood, was a rambling Federation house high on the side of a hill. My parents could only afford it because it was right in the middle of a planned freeway and would be demolished to make way for it. The roof leaked, the bathroom was primitive, plaster was falling off the walls. Only the most pressing repairs were ever done in the eight years we lived there. A bucket stood permanently beside the front door for when it rained. Mum made dinner every night in a kitchen that was just the closed-in end of the verandah, a narrow space hardly big enough to turn around in, managing on the old Kooka stove that was obsolete even when I was young.

We moved there in 1953 and for a few years the flat at the side—a DIY job done by Dad—was rented out to some young men always called 'the German boys'. Then, around 1955, when I was five, Grandma moved in. She was in her early seventies, but frail and pale like a much older person. At night I could hear her through the wall, coughing.

She came in and ate with us now and then, but more often she'd cook for herself, or Mum would take something through to her. I don't remember her often being with us as part of the family. She was aloof, thin, frowning, cranky. There was nothing cosily nanna-ish about her. I never saw her smile.

My clearest memory of Grandma is the day she came on me in the garden, busy with some game that involved crouching down rearranging dirt. She stood over me, from my point of view a tall length of disapproving grown-up topped by a stern face. When she suddenly asked, Do you love me, Cathy? I was bewildered. It wasn't the sort of question I'd ever been asked—I was growing up in a household full enough of love not to need to name it. I looked up at Grandma's unsmiling wrinkled face and said, No.

For years I told that story as a joke—the unlovable old woman demanding to be loved. Now I see the memory differently. She was asking the question because she wanted the answer to be *Yes*. Like everyone else, she longed to be loved and was unsure enough to have to ask. She was looking back over her life and—as surely we all do—feeling the pain of regret. I wish I'd thought of a kinder answer.

My mother often told me stories of her childhood, and in those stories Grandma was a cold, dominating mother. I heard many times how she'd bullied Mum into becoming a pharmacist, spending her days calculating and measuring and compounding, when what Mum loved was poetry and art: the mystery dimension of life that can't be calculated, can't be measured, can't be made into a pill to slip down easily. I heard about the loneliness that Grandma's restlessness had imposed on her children, sending them away to stay with distant family or strangers. There'd been so many moves that Mum claimed to have gone to fourteen different schools. In her telling, Grandma was uncaring, selfish, unloving. Even a bit mad.

I'd heard those stories often enough to shape a child's narrative about the two of them, one that drew a simple straight line from complaining about someone to not loving them. So when, early one morning, Mum came into my room, sat on the side of the bed, took my hand and said, Grandma's dead, Cathy, my impulse was to say, So why are you crying?

Did I say it? I was an insensitive little person and I might have. I hope not. I felt her searching my face for the same grief I could see on hers. I'd never seen Mum cry before. It frightened me. I didn't want to be drawn into an adult emotion I didn't understand.

Now I'm getting on for the age Dolly was when she died, and like all of us I've had things happen in my life, good and bad, and they've shown me a few things. I know now that you can criticise a person, complain about them, even think you hate them, but be bereft, confused, remorseful, pierced with unbearable regret when they die.

In her own last days, Mum asked again the question she'd so often come back to in talking about her childhood: *Why did my mother never love me?* I sat by her bed in the hospital and had no answer. I can see now that Mum's question came out of her own experience, but the answer to it had to be found in Dolly's. In a way this book is an attempt, after all this time, to come up with an answer to Mum's painful question. Perhaps it's also a different answer to the question Grandma asked me.

My mother left many fragments of memoir, and in 2015 I drew on them for a book about her life. It portrayed Grandma as my mother saw her, but as I researched for that book I found out more about the world Grandma had lived in. For the first time I started to see beyond Mum's account of her mother.

The only way we know many of those women born in the 1880s is from stiff, unreal old studio photos. Unless they were privileged or exceptional, most women vanished from the record. Their lives often can't be reconstructed beyond a few dates—their births and deaths, when their children were born—and maybe a recipe for drop scones or oxtail soup.

The events of my grandmother's life—drawn from family stories and research—are as I've told them here. But I've had to imagine my way into what she felt and thought about them, and no doubt I've got that wrong in all sorts of ways. It's only two generations ago, but Dolly's world seems a foreign country. In the old photos those women in their impossible clothes seem like another species, their lives unimaginable.

But those women are our foremothers. Their stories are our history. Those mostly silent, mostly unrecorded women are where we come from. If we'd been born when they were, our lives would have been theirs. At any time before the present (and continuing now in many parts of the world), if you were born clever and energetic, but female, you had to endure a life of injustice and frustration.

Dolly's was the transition generation. For women like her, born at the end of the nineteenth century, things were starting to change. Those women hacked out a space so that the women who came after them could have a different future. I wanted to bring one of them out from the silence of the past and give her a voice we could recognise. I wanted to let her speak to us as a living, breathing woman, complicated and contradictory: someone not all that different from us.

I haven't told the story of Dolly Maunder because she was unique or extraordinary. She wasn't, and that's the very reason I think her story is worth telling. It would have been repeated hundreds, even thousands of times: women doing their best, against every obstacle, to give their daughters a better chance at happiness than they'd had, and to find a corner of an unfriendly world where a woman could make a life for herself.

Thinking About Silences

DOLLY'S great-grandfather, Solomon Wiseman, was a convict who took many acres of Dharug land beside the river Deerubbin. Her grandfather, John Martin Davis, was a free settler who took many acres of Kamilaroi land beside the creek Carrabobbila. Her father, Thomas Henry Maunder, was an indentured labourer who took many acres of Kamilaroi land beside the mountain Warrigundi.

In their lifetimes Dolly and Bert lived on Country of the Kamilaroi, Guringai, Tharawal, Wiradjuri, Dharug, Gweagal, Gamaragal, Garigal, Kambuwal and Gundungerra. Their ashes are interred on Wallumedegal Country.

The lives of Dolly and her forebears all stand on the taking of land, but the family stories I drew on for this book are silent about that truth. They also record no awareness of the enduring sorrow all the taking meant—and means—for First Nations people. As Dolly's granddaughter, I want to acknowledge that silence and that sorrow. I've told one story here, but standing beside it is another.

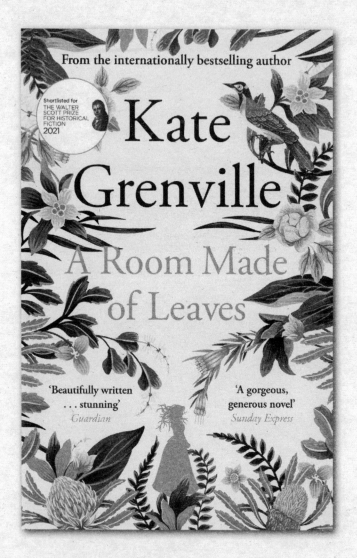

From the internationally bestselling author

Shortlisted for
THE WALTER
SCOTT PRIZE
FOR HISTORICAL
FICTION
2021

Kate Grenville

A Room Made of Leaves

'Beautifully written
... stunning'
Guardian

'A gorgeous,
generous novel'
Sunday Express

'Historical fiction at its best'
Good Housekeeping

CANON‖GATE

'An outstanding study of cultures in collision'
Guardian

CANON▌▌GATE

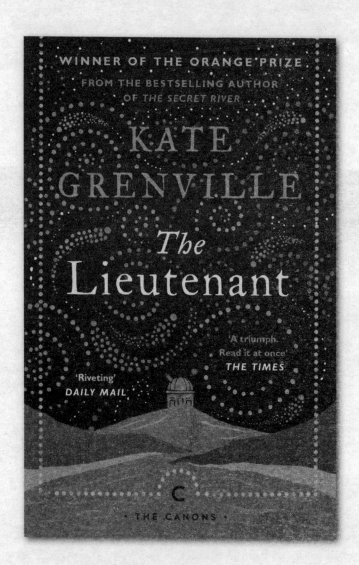

WINNER OF THE ORANGE PRIZE
FROM THE BESTSELLING AUTHOR
OF *THE SECRET RIVER*

KATE
GRENVILLE

The
Lieutenant

'A triumph.
Read it at once'
THE TIMES

'Riveting'
DAILY MAIL

C
· THE CANONS ·

'A triumph'
The Times

CANON❙❙GATE